Riley Pine is the comb...
contemporary romance...
them before. Expect de...
swoons. To stay up to ...
head on over to rileypine.com, for newsletters, book
details and more!

If you liked *My Royal Temptation*, why not try

Sweet Thing by Nicola Marsh
Make Me Want by Katee Robert
Ruined by Jackie Ashenden

Discover more at millsandboon.co.uk

MY ROYAL TEMPTATION

RILEY PINE

MILLS & BOON

First Published in Great Britain 2018
by Mills & Boon, an imprint of HarperCollins*Publishers*
1 London Bridge Street, London, SE1 9GF

© 2018 Riley Pine

ISBN 978-0-263-93209-6

MIX
Paper from
responsible sources
FSC www.fsc.org   **FSC C007454**

This book is produced from independently certified FSC™ paper
to ensure responsible forest management.
For more information visit www.harpercollins.co.uk/green.

Printed and bound in Spain
by CPI, Barcelona

CHAPTER ONE

Nikolai

IT'S NEVER IDEAL to wake up after a one-night stand to find a European boxing champion glaring at your bare ass. It's worse if the pissed-off guy in question happens to be a childhood best friend.

Scratch that…former best friend.

"Top of the morning." I wryly yank the hotel's satin sheet over my waist. A red thong is bunched on top of the unmade covers, right where I removed it with my teeth around midnight.

If looks could kill, Christian Wurtzer, Baron of Rosegate, would smite me faster than a lightning bolt hurled by an avenging god.

"You really are a first-rate bastard, aren't you, Nikolai?" He balled his hands into meaty fists, a useless gesture, because here in the Kingdom of Edenvale, it's illegal to strike a member of the royal family.

And as Prince Nikolai, third of his name, Duke of Westcraven, heir to the throne of Edenvale and our country's eminent blue-blooded bad boy, I fall square into the "no hitting allowed" category. Rules are often a nuisance in my world, but that particular clause has proved beneficial since reaching my maturity, especially in predicaments regarding the opposite sex.

"Bastard?" I scrub the morning scruff prickling my jaw with a yawn. "But I'm the mirror image of my dear sovereign father, and don't forget that my poor queen mother was forced to squeeze me out in front of an official court representative to ensure my legitimacy." There is a sharp localized pain in the vicinity of my heart; the twinge always accompanies a mention of my long-dead mother. She died bringing my youngest brother, Damien, into the world, the first life that banished asshole ever took.

"You've gone too far this time." Christian's warning growl yanks my attention back to the present moment. "This was my sister. You compromised her virtue."

Not the optimal moment to observe that he could give the ferocious bear stamped on his family crest a run for its money. Once our people were great hunters, the best swordsmen in Europe, as feared as the Vikings of old. Edenvale might be a small, landlocked kingdom, but we harbored a reputation as ruthless, lethal warriors. These days we're better known for luxury casinos, discreet banks and glamorous mountain hideaways. Edenvale is a high-altitude playground for the rich, the famous and those aspiring to the same.

"What will I tell my parents?" He rakes a hand through his blond hair, pacing the plush carpet. "Catriona is ruined. Her prospects for a marriage alliance are now nonexistent."

"Come, come. Ask any trust-fund baby in Ibiza. It's common knowledge that your precious little sister gave up her virtue well before I sunk my flag." If his family schemed to marry Cat off as a virgin, they lost that

chance years ago. Typical Rosegate sentiment to at-
tach significance to such an inconsequential thing as a
hymen. But they are an old-fashioned people. The re-
gional characteristic might be charming if their morals
weren't so fucking medieval.

Catriona Wurtzer stirs, snoring lightly, her pink lips
crooked into a satiated half smile. A hot pulse of lust
spreads through my sac. That luscious mouth pouts
from the cover of three different high-fashion magazines this month alone, and last night it worked over
my cock with such deep-throated skill that the interlude
nearly distracted me from this morning's royal duty.

I roll out of bed and slip on my tuxedo pants—
commando—and shrug into my dress shirt, not bothering with the twenty-four-karat-gold cuff links on the
nightstand. Catriona likes it rough, and the room was
trashed during our sleepover. Those expensive baubles
will serve as a more-than-adequate housekeeping tip.
It's time for me to return to the castle.

My father, the king, and my hag of a stepmother,
the current queen, have summoned me for a private
audience this morning at nine thirty sharp. This rare
audience doesn't mean anything good, which is why I
guzzled three-thousand-dollar-a-bottle champagne at
a gala benefit before burying myself balls deep into
the supermodel who happens to be my best friend's
little sister.

"Your family have been loyal subjects for over two
centuries. Based on this valued relationship, I shall issue
a royal decree. Huzzah, huzzah. All hail Catriona, the
realm's newest countess." I can't resist a smirk as I tack
on, "A new title for her trouble." As if bedding me was

a hardship. Which it wasn't. But what the hell? Let her add a castle to her four orgasms. I'm in a generous mood.

"Too kind, Highness." Christian nearly chokes on his words. He wants to beat my ass into Luxembourg, but the microstate of Rosegate has long been a disputed territory with Nightgardin, the country to the north and our ancient foe. The powerful Wurtzer family has been allied to mine for generations, and he knows—without reminder—three salient facts:

I'm an asshole, a leopard can't change his spots, and Edenvale's small but lethal military is the only thing protecting Rosegate against a Nightgardin power grab.

Revenge is a bitch.

Christian and I attended Swiss boarding school together and shared a dormitory room for five years. I love the guy like family, but he recently racked up too many gambling debts playing high-stakes blackjack. My sources say he decided to pay for them by selling titillating gossip about me to the tabloids. I'm not saying banging his hot sister is payback for his betrayal.

But I'm not saying it isn't, either.

A muscle twitches deep in his jaw, the same tic that would act up back when he'd pour over his calculus lessons during late-night study sessions. I'm sure he'd love to order me to "do the right thing" and stick a ring on his sister's finger. But alas, only one of us carries an invitation-only Black Amex card with no preset limits.

Limits are for those who need them. I am no such man.

People can think I'm an arrogant ass all they want. They're right. But at least I'm a consistent asshole. Fuck with me and I fuck back. No hard feelings. It's how the people on top stay on top. And I can make it good.

Or I can make it hurt.

For those who beg nicely—I can make it both.

Got to say, being a prince is full of perks in all ways but one—I still answer to the king. It's not my throne…yet.

I glance in the gilded mirror on my way out the door. Yep, still me. Bed-rumpled jet-black hair, a roguish mouth and gunmetal gray eyes. I clock in at six foot four and possess stamina for days. Last year I came in number one on a list of the world's sexiest royals. The only thing surprising was that it was the first year it happened. Way I see it, Prince Harry over in jolly old England can eat his ginger heart out.

"For Christ's sake. Wake up, Catriona," Christian orders his sister as I exit the room. I outpace the unfolding drama and stride down the hotel hallway, hitting the button on the penthouse's private elevator. My bodyguard, X, waits in the Rolls. He's been idling there all night. He's used to it.

I slide into the back seat without a word.

A language lesson plays on the sound system—Mandarin Chinese. X collects languages like he does medieval knives. Not my first choice for fun, but to each his own.

"To the castle, Sire?" he asks over the intercom, turning off the stereo. I remove my sunglasses from my pocket. Daylight reflects from the snow on the high mountain peaks. My growing headache isn't in the mood for good weather.

"Home sweet home." I slather sarcasm on my affirmative and slide on the shades to avoid the summer sun.

As X starts the engine, I reach into the minibar and

pluck out a handful of miniature cognac bottles. By the time we cross the moat, I toss the fifth empty on the pile by my feet. But the liquor does jack shit to dull the sharp pain in my gut.

Fine. It was an unforgivable move to fuck my best friend's little sister—revenge or no—but I'm sure as shit no Prince Charming.

Kate

I spread my hands across my pleated skirt, then think better of it and rest them atop the leather folder that sits on the table. If I wanted to, I could relax, even luxuriate in the high-backed, cushioned chair, no doubt made of the same buttery leather as the folder in front of me. But it's not exactly easy when you're sitting at a twenty-foot-long mahogany table in one of many rooms at the Palace Edenvale.

It wasn't like I hadn't been here before, but I don't think a prep-school tour counts the same as an invitation that came hand-delivered by a royal herald. The envelope was even closed with one of those fancy wax seals.

Dear Miss Katherine Winter,
Your presence is requested at Palace Edenvale at 9:30 a.m. tomorrow morning. Please come unattended and plan on clearing your schedule for the remainder of the day. Your audience with the king and queen must be kept private. Tell no one where you are going, and after you've been, tell no one what transpires within the palace walls until—should they request your ser-

vices further—the king, queen and yourself enter into contract.

The royal family appreciates you honoring your duty and complying with the above requests.

I huff out a laugh, which echoes in the empty room. *Requests.* As if I had any choice once I broke the royal seal. Sure, Your Highnesses, I'll clear my day. Of course, my illustrious rulers, I'll keep my visit to the palace a secret. Not because of any damned duty, though. If there is one thing I value, it's my business and my independence. I am determined to keep the former and as much of the latter as possible, and if that means zipping my lips about my *royal audience*, fine by me.

There better at least be some sort of monetary compensation for this—this—*request*. God knows my sister and I need it. Our savings account has dipped into the red with Gran's mounting medical bills, which has sent my internal stress thermometer in the exact opposite direction.

I glance at the thin gold bracelet on my wrist, an eighteenth-birthday gift from my beloved grandmother, back in happier times. Back when she still remembered my name.

I swallow the threat of tears. This is hardly the time or the place to wallow in my personal woes.

"We won't lose the apartment." The words are a mantra. "And we'll still be able to take care of Gran."

I figure if I say the words enough, they'll be true. So I open my mouth once more to repeat the statements, but the conference-room doors part with a whoosh, and my worry fades into the distance as the same formal-looking man who delivered my invitation steps over the threshold and announces my small country's rulers in a booming voice.

"All rise for His Highness, King Nikolai of Edenvale, and Her Eminence, Queen Adele."

The herald proclaims the royal couple as if they are entering an arena, and I, of course, shoot to my feet. My first instinct is to bow or curtsy, but neither one of them spares me so much as a passing glance. Yet I'm the only one in the room. I've been requested for a private audience with the *monarchy*, and they don't even deign to look at me.

Still, I wait for the attendants who trail behind the pair to pull out two chairs at the head of the table. I wait some more as they lower themselves into the plush leather seats. And as I'm about to do the same, a man wearing half a tuxedo bursts through the doors still tucking in his wrinkled dress shirt.

He winks in my direction, flashing a knavish grin before turning his attention to the king and queen.

"Sorry I'm late," he says, checking a nonexistent watch on his wrist. Then he kisses the queen on the cheek while the king, a salt-and-pepper version of the young man, simply gives his son—Prince Nikolai— a pointed look.

While his parents—make that father and stepmother— take residence at the far head of the table, the prince sits across from me and flips open the embossed folder in front of him.

"So," he says, sprawling in his chair and thumbing through the folder's contents, "what fire are we putting out this morning?"

He runs a hand through his black hair, and I squirm

involuntarily in my seat. Sure, I've seen photos of him before. Prince Nikolai's image has graced the front page of the tabloids almost weekly since he came of age. But that sort of sensationalism has never been my thing. I wasn't the preteen with pictures of the teen heartthrob prince on my wall. I didn't wallpaper my computer's desktop with his devil-may-care smile, no matter how gorgeous he was.

And he *was*. Even then.

But he was also a grade-A asshole. Even then.

And from the looks of things—from the colorful headlines that always seem to feature Prince Nikolai's name—it doesn't seem like anything is changing soon.

Still, when those slate-colored eyes look up from the folder and meet mine, I squirm again. He was handsome in photos and the few times I've seen him on television. Not that I watch much of that celebrity crap that's thrown in the public's face on a daily basis. But I'm not prepared for my reaction to the prince in the flesh.

He is nothing short of dazzling.

My lungs revolt, unable to take a deep breath even though I need air badly.

And as if it isn't enough that he has some sort of superpower effect between my legs, I feel my nipples stand at attention against the lace of my bra. Thank God I'd had the forethought to keep my suit jacket buttoned.

"Nikolai—" the queen begins, but the prince holds up a finger as he returns to scanning the contents of the folder—the one I have been waiting for permission to examine myself. Apparently, the rumors are true—

stepmother and stepson do not get on as they should. That explains the blatant disrespect.

His shuttered gaze roams the first page, then the second, and several more after that. I watch as his father crosses his arms and humors his son with a look that says no matter what antics the prince displays, the king will have the final word.

Prince Nikolai slams the folder closed and lets out a raucous laugh.

"Please, Nikolai," the king says, steepling his fingers in front of him. "Do tell us what you find so amusing."

The queen rests a hand on her husband's forearm, but the man's icy gaze remains directed at his son. All I do is stare, my head bobbing like I'm watching a tennis match in slow motion.

The prince narrows his eyes, pinning them on me, and my core tightens in disobedient response.

He takes his sweet time scrutinizing me, the corner of his mouth quirked in a crooked grin. Then he splays his hands on the table, leaning forward so that he's close enough for me to smell the tang of alcohol on his breath.

"I find it hilarious," the prince says with an edge to his words, "that you not only expect me to marry but that you think Little Miss Matchmaker-Dot-Com is the one to take care of the job. I mean, why not open me a royal Tinder account and be done with it?"

He has the nerve to sneer at me and my career? Oh, hell no.

Red-hot anger replaces that sensual tightening in my core.

The prince pushes from the table and smooths out

his wrinkled shirt. "Father. Stepmother. As always, it's a pleasure to see you both." He doesn't hide his sarcasm.

On instinct, I stand as he rounds the table, my cheeks blazing with repressed fury.

"I—I am not some dot-com organization. My matches are personal, well thought out…" I sputter as it sinks in not only what I've been called here to do but that my client is anything but willing.

"Save it, sweetheart," he says. "I'd sooner fuck you than let you arrange my nuptials."

The queen gasps, and King Nikolai slams his fist on the table.

"Enough," the older man says, the finality of his authority dripping from the word. "Benedict is entering the priesthood. Damien is banished. If you do not marry with the intent to produce an heir, the throne falls out of the immediate family and to your cousin Ingrid. You will not fault on your duty."

The muscle in the prince's jaw pulses. "That's right, Father. I've had enough." His penetrating stare, though, stays on me the whole time. That's when he leans in, hot breath on my cheek. "And you'd enjoy every goddamn second of it," he whispers. "The word *enough* won't even exist in your vocabulary."

He bows toward his visibly shaken parents before making his dramatic exit.

I give myself a mental pat on the back for at least believing the stories.

The prince *is* a grade-A asshole.

My soaked panties, on the other hand, apparently did not receive the memo.

Perhaps they're waiting for one with the royal seal.

CHAPTER TWO

Nikolai

"MARRIAGE? THAT'S IT, Father has lost his goddamn mind," I mutter, ducking into the unobtrusive staircase, the quickest escape route out of the palace. Two floors down a young servant in a black dress and white apron takes one look at me and nearly drops the silver tray she carries, one laden with teapots, fine china and six different cakes. My mood is so foul that I ignore her alarmed squeal and don't even smooth the situation over with a flirtatious wink.

She must have been assigned catering duty for the ambush upstairs, the one where my father invoked the ancient laws of our realm.

Sweat breaks out on my hairline. A sour taste fills my mouth.

My twenty-ninth birthday is just around the corner.

I am the heir to the crown.

The Royal Marriage Decree of 1674 declared that the Edenvale heir must wed before sundown on his or her twenty-ninth birthday or their claim is null and void. Plus, an Edenvale heir had to marry someone of aristocratic blood. My future bride doesn't have to be

a citizen of my country, but she does need to be no-
bility. Other than that, the requirements are simple:
free consent.

Sounds easy enough. Except for the part where I'm
not the marrying kind.

I reach the bottom of the stairs and draw a lung-
searing breath before pushing through the exit that
leads to the castle grounds.

Of course I know about the marriage decree. I
memorized Edenvale proclamations and laws alongside my ABCs. But this is the twenty-first century. I
never dared believe that Father would enforce that ar-
cane law any more than he would the one about how no
high ministers could enter the palace wearing purple,
or how hunting on royal lands was a hangable offense.

Don't even get me started on the decree prohibit-
ing anal sex.

Hell, I tapped the back door of a hotel heiress in
the castle's highest tower last week. Not something I
normally do, but she offered, and I sure as shit wasn't
going to turn it down. Not my favorite position, but
sex is like pizza in Naples. Even if it's not great, it's
still damn good.

The castle grounds are perfectly manicured with
hedges cut into topiaries of rabbits and swans. Father
enjoys indulging his whimsical side.

The morning sun scalds my neck.

"Sire, Sire, please, wait!" a woman cries behind me.
Then she mutters under her breath how hard it is to
run in heels.

My molars grind with enough force that it's a mir-
acle they don't shatter. I've heard that lilting voice

before—the auburn-haired woman from the match-making service that my father hired.

Marriage decree aside, this situation—them hiring a matchmaking service—is the biggest insult of all. As if I need any goddamn help finding a willing woman.

"Sire!"

I should wait. Chivalry and all that. But remember the part about how I'm no Prince Charming?

I veer into the maze, kicking at stones in the gravel path. Fuck being a gentleman. I turn left, then right, then left again. The walls surrounding me are twelve feet high and covered in leaves. This maze might be the largest in Europe, but it was my childhood playground. I always know the way out. Time to ditch this tenacious matchmaker and figure out a plan to avoid getting tied in unholy matrimony.

That's when I hear it.

A snap, quickly followed by a sound like someone trying not to cry out.

Shit.

She's fallen over.

Not a surprise. I caught a glimpse of her precarious five-inch stilettos when she crossed her legs upstairs in the castle hall and this path is rocky and uneven.

I also caught an eyeful of a toned calf that connected to a perfectly curving thigh. That was the best part of the meeting. Before I glanced at the folder on the table and read the gold-embossed title: Happy Endings Matchmaking Services: Making Dreams a Reality.

A cool mountain breeze brushes my face. I pause. Debating. I want to keep going. I even take a step. It's not like I asked her to give chase. She saw that I didn't need her advice. That I didn't want her professional services. Yet she insisted on pursuing me of her own free will. This is her own fault. I owe the woman—a total stranger—nothing.

The image of that exquisite creamy thigh flashes behind my eyes, this time draped over my shoulder.

Okay. Correction. I don't want her in a *professional* capacity.

My shoulders slump. No matter what my instincts demand, I can't abandon an injured woman alone in the maze.

Before I know it, I'm backtracking. It takes less than thirty seconds to find her.

She's kicked off that lethal-looking shoe and sits rubbing a swelling ankle. Her toes are painted a glossy classic red.

Okay, damn. I like that.

Her lips are flawless, painted in exactly the same shade.

I like that even better.

I'd like it best streaking my shaft.

My cock twitches in agreement.

Fuck. This matchmaker—and maddeningly sexy woman—is the enemy. But try telling that to my ass-hole dick. Sometimes an overactive libido comes with serious drawbacks.

Then her gaze fixes on my face, and with one look at those tear-filled baby blues, my brain fucking flatlines.

Kate

It takes everything for me to hold my prince's fixed stare, not to wince at the white-hot pain in my ankle.

But there is no way I'm letting this guy—prince or otherwise—get the best of me.

"You okay?" he asks.

"Of course not." I glance at my ivory skirt, the side slit ripped even higher. I'm also sure my ass is one big grass stain. And let's not even discuss the hair. I'd gone for professional with the French twist, but now my auburn waves hang in my face, which is probably for the best. His steely gaze is too close.

"Just—show me the way out," I say, attempting to push myself up, but as soon as I put pressure on my bare foot, my knees buckle and I almost hit the ground again.

Almost. Because Nikolai Lorentz, Prince of Edenvale and heir to the throne, catches me.

"Shit," he hisses. "You *are* hurt."

"And you smell like you hit a limousine minibar," I say, trying to cover my reaction to his hands on me with disdain.

But my breath still quickens. He carries me with a concern I can feel in every nerve of my body.

"It was a Rolls, but you're very perceptive, Miss—"

"Winter," I say, having no choice but to throw my arms around his neck for purchase, my broken shoe still dangling from my fingers.

"Aha," he says, that devilish grin taking over his features. "Have you read *Romeo and Juliet*? Doesn't Juliet ask what's in a name?" He begins to walk.

My cheeks grow hot, and the tips of his fingers—his palm where it touches the bare skin of my thigh—sends sparks right through me.

I clear my throat. "You read Shakespeare?" I ask, though it's obvious.

"You're as icy as your name implies."

I huff out a breath and push as far from him as I can while the rogue still has me in his arms.

"I'm no such thing! *You—you're* the one who likened my services to a dating website. My work is nuanced and relies on personal metrics and psychology, thank you very much. You're also the one who just cost me a day's work. So pardon me if I'm not exactly warming to your famous *charm*."

He stops dead in his tracks. We're still in the maze, and I can't tell if we're any closer to making it out of here or if he's taken us deeper.

His eyes dart in every direction, as if he's checking for intruders, before they land on mine. Stone gray and burning with intent, I can't look away if I try.

"I *will not* marry," he says, his voice cool and even. "Is that understood?"

I nod. "And I will *not* walk away from this job."

"Then I guess we're at an impasse."

The air between us is warm, charged with the mingling of our breaths. His skin against mine sizzles. My head tells me that everything I'm feeling is wrong, but the physical need brewing inside me throbs at my core.

I haven't been with a man since my fiancé, Jean-Luc, died BASE jumping in Alaska. He was the love of my life, but he loved the thrill of adrenaline more than me. Afterward, I joined my big sister Madeline's business to devote my life to what I was denied: a happy ending.

It had been two long, careful years of self-denial and occasionally my own hand. Before that it had only ever been Jean-Luc.

But the hand against me now is big, strong and unfamiliar. All it would take is his fingers sliding an inch more, and he'd *feel* that need, wet and pulsing.

He swallows, and I watch his Adam's apple bob. That's all it takes to let me know that whatever this is, it's not only me.

Maybe this is what it feels like to live in the moment, take a risk, something I never let myself do because I had to be careful for both of us. I had to move in with Madeline to save on rent. Never have I let myself simply *want*.

But this stranger's hands on me are warm. Strong. And for a second I imagine what they could do. It's intoxicating, this growing need and the possibility of satisfying it right here and now. I feel drunk and squirm in his grasp, hoping he'll simply think I'm readjusting myself in his arms, but I miscalculate and my lips brush against his.

He sucks in a breath, and this makes me grin.

"I *don't* like you," I say. Truer words have never been spoken.

"Likewise," he answers, his voice low and rough.

All my life I've played it safe, and where did it get me? Lost and alone. But this man exudes raw power, a power that draws me into his orbit, a pull stronger than gravity. I feel myself inching toward some sort of internal cliff, and the woman I thought I was relinquishes control.

"You said you'd sooner fuck me than let me arrange your nuptials."

He nods. "I certainly did."

I lean close to his ear, nip at his lobe, and step across the line of comfort I've hidden behind for far too long and whisper, "It's *sooner*."

I expect a savage response, but instead I feel him adjust his hands, and then I gasp as his thumb hits the crease of my panties.

That's all it takes. I leap off the cliff with a whimper of need and straight into pure pleasure.

He growls.

"You're fucking soaked." He drops to his knees, still holding me like I'm precious cargo, and lays me gently on the grass. "And I want to drink every last sweet drop."

Without another word, he hikes my skirt up and slides my panties down my thighs, over my knees and then off. I feel them snag on the heel of my remaining shoe but don't care. He shoves them in the pocket of his pants, and I know I'm not getting them back. The thought makes me giddy, and I writhe under his gaze.

"Now, Nikolai," I say, and he levels me with his grin.

The next thing I know, my hands are tangled in that jet-black hair as he licks the length of my folds from bottom to top until his tongue swirls around my swollen clit.

I moan and buck against him as he sucks me between his lips. I relish the feel of his stubble against my thighs, the slight pain only heightening my pleasure.

"Use fingers," I command, and he obeys immediately.

One finger plunges deep while he continues to take his fill with his mouth. Then a second joins the first, and my vision clouds with stars. My body bucks with shivers of reaction.

"God, I wish you could fuck me," I say, daring to voice what I long for—what I've gone without for what seems like an eternity. I try and fail not to whimper as he reaches a spot inside me that almost makes me black out.

Two years. It's been two freaking years since a man has touched me. The thought—coupled with his hands on me, in me—threatens to unleash something more than just the adrenaline rush, but I swallow the impending wave of emotion. Because that's not what this is about. These feelings aren't for the prince.

He peeks from between my legs and slides his fingers from my aching pussy. He takes care in licking each one clean.

"You said it was sooner, sweetheart, and I'm *always* prepared for sooner." From the pocket that does not hold my ruined panties, he pulls a foil packet and holds it up for me to see. "Your wish is my command."

CHAPTER THREE

Nikolai

HER TASTE IS ADDICTIVE—honey, salt and rainwater. I hate the idea of matchmaking. But matchmakers? I take my time drinking in the woman panting on the grass, her conservative blouse opened a button too far, exposing delicate white lace, creamy skin and lush, womanly curves.

Yes. I believe I could learn to like matchmakers.

"Sire. Hurry." She stares through a fringe of dark, thick lashes. Her red lipstick is smudging off her plump lower lip. I'm responsible for that, and the fact draws my balls tight against my engorged cock, clearly outlined through the panel of my tux pants. My muscles ripple with suppressed need.

I fold my arms, making an elaborate show of regarding the condom foil, and set my face into my trademark arrogant sneer. It's my mask. The one the public expects a prince to wear, especially a prince with the world at his feet. It comes easy as instinct, which is good because I am not used to being unsettled. And this woman is—*unsettling*.

"Interesting business you run." I lower my voice to a sensual drawl.

"No, not mine. I mean… I am not… It's not mine… um… It's my sister's…her business," she babbles, skimming one hand over the ragged tear in her prim skirt, the one currently offering me an eyeful of the thighs I'd feasted on. Her eyes darken, pupils dilating at my blatant appraisal.

"And do you provide these *services*—" I clear my throat and raise an insinuating eyebrow "—to every client?"

A dusky rose color flushes the skin of her throat as she catches my insinuation. She's pissed. Angry and turned on, my favorite combination in a woman. Hate fucking has all of the fun and none of the responsibility.

"Of course not," she snaps.

I dip a finger between my lips and give it a long lazy suck. The muscles in my neck cord. It still tastes like her. My mouth waters. "Mmm-hmm. Methinks the lady doth protest too much."

"Damn it." A tear spills from the corner of one gorgeous eye, trickles along her high cheekbone. "I don't know what came over me."

My hands twitch to comfort her. Christ. I did not see that response coming. I should regroup, charm her thighs open and plunge into her from behind, working her fancy hairdo and composure loose in brutal doggystyle strokes. Bet it would make her bum ankle feel a lot better than two ibuprofens and an ice pack.

So why am I pocketing the condom? Or brushing a wayward lock of hair on her forehead.

"Look. It's been…" She flinches from my touch with a bitter laugh. "A while. And you…well, you're royal

sex on a stick. It's a lot for a normal person to take in."
She closes the gaping button on her shirt. "An error in
judgment that won't happen again."

Looks like I'm not the only one who slaps on a
mask when the going gets tough. In a blink of an eye
my feisty sex kitten has retracted her claws and is now
back to Miss Prim and Proper.

"Pity," I rumble, trying not to appear disconcerted.
"Errors in judgment happen to be my specialty." I take
my time adjusting my cock, the proud, hard length
straining inside my pants.

The point of her pink tongue makes a quick appear-
ance, dabs her lower lip. The kitten reemerges for a
second. "You do seem quite...specialized."

"And you have once again proven my long-tested
theory correct."

"Which is?"

I tap the tip of her nose with my index finger. "Inside every good girl is a bad girl waiting to get out."

She fingers her pearl choker. "I'm not going to argue
with you there." Her laugh is high-pitched—nervous.
"I've always been the good girl. Oral in a royal maze
is a first and so, *so* not me."

I believe her. She looks like an angel. I might have
sucked her sweet clit, but those doe-like eyes speak to
nothing but innocence. That's when I'm slammed by a
vision of a woman naked in my bed, long legs spread
wide, hiding nothing, each pink honeyed fold exposed
for my pleasure. Her delicate wrists and ankles bound
by thick ropes of pearl.

I blink. My shoulders go rigid. I've never invited a
woman into my royal bed. The west wing of the palace is my personal sanctuary. No one is welcome there

save for my brother Benedict. Not my dalliances. And not my father or stepmother. It's the only place that is just for me. Where I can be—*me*.

The world gets my dick. No one has a right to my soul.

"This was obviously a mistake," she murmurs to herself before rising unsteadily. "We got off on the wrong foot."

"*You* got off on the wrong foot." I nod at her bare right foot, the one on which she can barely place any weight, and I offer her my arm. She takes it, but not before rolling her eyes. "We got off on more than that," I add. My cock jumps like a dog hungry for a treat. "At least *you* did."

She sniffs. Who'd imagine this ice queen could melt into such a passionate, bright, fiery lover?

Interesting.

She limps but is able to hold her own now. I like to think it has something to do with my talent between her legs, that my skillful tongue has a healing effect. I guide her out of the maze. Grass stains mar her perfectly tailored ivory skirt, a visible reminder of what we just did, and just like that, I'm hard as a rock again.

"From the tabloids," she says, "it sounds like you won't suffer for long. Tell me, how long has it been since you were inside a woman?"

I shrug with studied nonchalance. "Mouth or pussy?"

She gasps as my words sink in.

I pretend to count my fingers. "Six hours for pussy. Seven for her mouth. Give or take fifteen minutes. And if her brother hadn't barged in on us this morning, I'm guessing those numbers would be significantly smaller."

"You're a pig." Her brows slam together. "A rutting, depraved boar."

"No. I'm a prince." I draw myself to full height. "*Your* prince."

"And I'm here in service to my king." She juts out her jaw, gaze unbowed, refusing to cave at my power play. "Sire, you are my client. It's been royally commanded by your father and my liege lord, which means we need to get to work. I will return tomorrow to do your personality profile."

"My what?"

"It's protocol for all our clients." There is a note of finality in her clipped tone. She means business.

I click my tongue, half annoyed and half impressed. "You'll never marry me off, sweetheart."

"Tell that to my matchmaking success rate of 100%." She offers a smug smile. "See you tomorrow, Highness."

Once out of the maze, she releases my arm and continues alone. But she's still injured, so her haughty exit falls flat, even as she takes off her other shoe. I bite back a laugh before realizing the joke is on me. Because guess who still has a hard-on the size of the Matterhorn?

Still, I should follow her to the castle lest she goes to the tabloids with some trumped-up story about how poorly she was treated on palace property.

"I am fine to proceed alone," she says, reading my thoughts. An unsettling experience.

"I'm afraid I must insist," I say, taking the few steps needed to catch up to her.

"Please." Her composure slips a notch. The mask

not fully secure. "I—I need a moment alone." A sign this unexpected dalliance affected her, as well.

She turns and makes her way toward the palace gates, clutching her heels, only the slightest limp still evident. Miss Winter has spunk. I'll give her that.

A woman like this could bring a less controlled man to his knees. Good thing that I'm no such man. This angel is more dangerous than any devil.

Kate

I don't care if it hurts to walk. Nothing is more important than distance. And by distance I mean space between me and Nikolai Lorentz.

The only problem? When I slip through the gates onto the main grounds, I can't get to the front of the castle without swimming the moat.

Good Lord. He lives in a palace. With a moat. And I almost slept with him in a freaking maze. I begged the prince of our realm to *fuck me* as I lay in the grass with my skirt hiked up over my hips. What the hell is wrong with me? I don't *fuck* anybody. I have lovely, meaningful sex with men who love and care for me— and who put a ring on it. At least, I did have that once.

As I contemplate my next move, an older man— probably in his late thirties—approaches me from a nearby garden.

"Pardon me, Miss Winter, but I have been instructed to take you home."

I shake my head. "No, thank you. That won't be necessary. If you could point me toward the most direct route to the main road, I'm sure I can get a taxi."

I look behind me, expecting to see Nikolai approaching, but he's nowhere to be found.

"Miss, there is no direct route to the main road other than through the palace." He looks me up and down. "And I am assuming you'd like to make a discreet exit?"

I sigh and cling to the last shred of my dignity, holding my head high even as my just-been-finger-fucked hair falls into my face.

"I'm quite content walking through the palace…" But I trail off as I note myself gesturing with my shoes in my hands—as threads from my torn skirt tickle my thigh—and I immediately deflate.

"So…you were instructed to take me home?"

The man nods, the hints of silver in his dark hair glinting in the sun, and it's only now that I realize his impeccably tailored suit, his straightened spine and hands clasped in front of his hips. His jaw is chiseled and his brown eyes are dark and knowing. He is not royalty. I can tell that much. But he exudes an undisputable authority nonetheless.

"Yes, Miss. His Royal Highness the Prince texted me with the order to see you home safely. I can lead you through the kitchen and out the servants' exit to avoid any unpleasant encounters upon your departure."

I hold out my arms, shoes dangling from my index fingers. "I guess I'm not in any shape to run into the king and queen again, especially if I want to keep this job."

The man doesn't even crack a smile but instead offers me a single nod.

"This way, Miss." He motions toward the garden from which he came.

I limp in his direction, trying not to read into the prince's gesture of making sure I get home safely. There is no way Nikolai Lorentz cares what happens between us from here on out other than him opposing my very being here.

"You can call me Kate," I say, once I reach his side and he holds out an arm. I grab both of my shoes with my right hand and take his arm with my left—not because I need to but because it would seem rude to decline.

I breathe in sharply as my hand grips muscle so tight and corded that I can feel it through his suit.

"As you wish, Miss Kate," he says, and I roll my eyes.

"Maybe you could drop the *Miss* altogether? Makes me sound like a prim-and-proper governess." I let out a nervous laugh. What just transpired between me and the heir apparent was *not* behavior becoming of a governess. Or the me I thought I knew, for that matter.

"As you wish, *Kate*," he says, his voice devoid of any hint of emotion.

"You got a name?" I ask as he pushes open a door hidden in the brick of the palace's side wall.

"His Highness calls me X," he says, ushering me inside a small corridor. The servants' quarters, no doubt.

"What do your friends and family call you?" I ask.

He clears his throat. "I have neither, Miss—my apologies—*Kate*."

My stomach sinks at the thought as he leads me through a white six-panel door. But I forget the heartbreaking answer just as quickly as we enter an enormous kitchen and my senses are assaulted in the best possible way. The aroma of garlic wafts in our direction, and my mouth immediately waters. I skipped breakfast this morning because—hello—I was ordered to the palace. Who can eat with that kind of pressure? And now that I'd been satiated in a whole other way entirely, I was famished. There's also something sweet in the air, a richness I can almost taste.

"Would you like one for the road, Miss?" A woman covered in a white apron spins from where she's plating macarons from a baking pan onto a three-tiered plate.

I swallow before I start to drool. "Please," I say, and she grabs a small saucer from beneath the island where she works and serves me *five* of the delicious-looking confections.

"Our secret," she says with a wink and a smile, handing my bounty to X. The man simply nods and continues piloting me toward the exit.

The next thing I know, I'm sitting in the luxury of a Rolls-Royce, a plate of macarons in my lap, and an ice pack on my ankle—also, according to X, ordered by the prince. But the older man speaks no more as he pulls free of the palace gates, out onto the main thoroughfare and toward the apartment I share with my sister in the heart of town.

As I sit here, the breeze of the car's open windows hits me right up the bottom of my skirt, and I'm reminded of the fact that not only am I going commando, but also my underwear is bunched in the Prince of Edenvale's pocket.

Just swallow me up, world, because I am too much of a cliché to exist. I can see the tabloid headline now:

Royal Touch Wakes Celibate Woman's Libido

It isn't that I've ignored the whole libido thing. I have an active imagination and a pretty stellar showerhead. It's not like I've gone completely without. But the first time I go *with* is not supposed to be with my future king, and it certainly isn't supposed to unleash a torrent of pent-up emotion, not when a pint of chocolate gelato is nowhere in sight.

I close my eyes and try to erase the image of him grinning before he went down on me, but it turns out that eyes open, closed, crossed or whatever still draw the same picture—Nikolai Lorentz pleasuring me and taking pleasure in doing so.

And then when I'd called our little maze dalliance a mistake, he'd ordered his driver to take care of me— right down to a ride in his private car and the cool pack soothing the throb in my twisted ankle.

Maybe I am a cliché, something I never thought I'd be. But then again, maybe Prince Nikolai, Duke of Westcraven, isn't what I'd had in mind, either.

I pop a golden lemon macaron into my mouth and moan with pleasure.

Nope. Not what I had in mind at all.

CHAPTER FOUR

Nikolai

NOTHING LIKE A scalding hot shower after a night of rough sex with your former best friend's little sister, followed by impromptu cunnilingus in the palace maze with the matchmaker bankrolled by your father to find your future queen.

It's been a strange twenty-four hours.

I rock my head back. Forget a standard showerhead. I custom designed my own personal waterfall. My groan bounces off the slate tiles as my tense muscles relax in the spray. Shit yeah. This feels good. Almost as good as it did to be on my knees between Miss Winter's sweet thighs. I chuckle to myself. Me. On my knees before a woman. Can't remember the last time that happened.

A visceral memory flies in from the outer reaches of my subconscious and slams my gut with the intensity of an earth-ending meteor.

There once had been a woman who brought me to my knees. But I wasn't much past a boy then. Now I'm all man with a kingdom that's mine for the taking.

I grab a bottle of my favorite Tom Ford body wash

and pour a generous dollop in my palm. There's one thing that will relax me. Using the wash as lube, I thrust my cock into my hand in slow, lazy strokes before upgrading to my tried-and-true fist-over-fist technique, my length enough that one hand can never do the job. My ass clenches as I give over to the build.

Here's a fact. No woman, no matter how expert a lover, can touch a guy better than he touches himself. I'm captain of my own fucking ship. Yet here I am, imagining innocent, angel-faced Kate and her beautiful hands—small, delicate, manicured. I picture her grabbing me at the root, and I let out a guttural groan. What is it about this stranger that drives me crazy enough for her to invade my thoughts like this? Every nerve ending in my shaft is ready to burst into flames.

That's when I remember.

I still have her panties in my pocket. I step out of the shower, not giving two shits about getting the floor wet, and yank them from my tuxedo pants. The delicate ivory is pale in my tanned hand. On instinct, I lift them to my face and inhale the elegant French lace. My eyes roll. Beguiling. I'm a goddam pussy connoisseur, and this is the equivalent to uncorking a bottle of Château Mouton Rothschild 1945. I keep a case in my wine cellar, each bottle valued at twenty-five thousand euros.

I clutch the matchmaker's panties in one hand and step back in the shower, working over my cock with increased urgency as her scent overpowers my senses. Sweat breaks out across my chest and is washed away in a torrent of steamy water.

There are those who get intimidated by winery tasting rooms, but it's simple. A good vintage is composed of four things: fruits, acids, tannins and sugars. Young tannins can make the mouth pucker, leave your tongue dry. Left over time it increases in complexity, covering your palate with a signature silkiness. My palate is exceptional, able to identify a vintage by the subtle yet complex notes of coffee, chocolate, blackberry and spice.

Women are much the same. Each with her own nuances. And Kate Winter is in a class all her own. Fruity, with a hint of cherry, but also darker, more intriguing notes, such as to be found in a rich forest floor. She is the fruit of the earth, and I'm starving for the harvest.

A few more strokes and I'm poised on the edge, and then I pitch over, shattering into the most mind-numbing orgasm in a decade. For a moment, I wonder if I'm struck blind. Then the world returns, and I wash my hands, turn off the spray and grab a towel for my waist.

It takes me five minutes to regain my breath. After an intense, almost holy, experience like that, there is only one place to go—my brother, the saint.

Benedict will enter the priesthood. As a virgin.

Fucking crazy, right? My father bursts with pride at the fact he has a son destined for the priesthood and St. Egbert Abbey. To me, it's a fate worse than hell, and besides, it's more pressure. Benedict's put our bloodline at risk given that I'm the heir and he's the spare. My youngest brother, Damien, doesn't factor into the equation as he is banished and thereby removed from the line of succession. If I screw up here, the kingdom could pass from my family to my cousin Ingrid. She is a nice enough girl, and I don't mean that dismissively. She is ten years old.

I shove on a pair of sweatpants, lace up my running

shoes and catch my reflection in the window. I look like a debauched lord of the underworld.

Reflections on my banished brother Damien spiral me into a brooding darkness. The latest rumors claim that he resides half-time in London and the rest over in America. He could build a hermetically sealed tower in Madagascar for all I care, and it would still be too goddamn close. My family is like the setup to a bad joke: a commitment-phobic heir to the throne, a virgin almost-priest, and a black sheep all walk into a bar…

I jog through the quiet palace, past row after row of ancient ancestors appraising me from gilded frames. Do they wonder if I'll ever measure up? If I'll fulfill my legacy? Damn these black thoughts to hell. I get outside and run until my lungs are near bursting. On the edge of the grounds, near the Royal River, is the tower where my brother lives. He calls it his sanctuary, and he's not wrong. Poor bastard might not use his cock, but he has peace. And he deserves it because I don't say bastard lightly.

There isn't conclusive proof, but there are many rumors that my mother took a brief liking to the head of her secret-service detail while my father was at a UN summit. The only evidence? My brother's piercing green eyes—neither my mother's nor my father's.

I try the door.

"It's locked, Sir," a formal male voice calls out.

I turn to find X there, watching me with his usual impenetrable expression. One would think that after years of him appearing by my side without setting off so much as a floorboard creak, I would be used to his stealth. But it still unnerves me every time.

"I'm afraid Mr. Benedict was called away on urgent business."

"Where to?" I ask.

"Vatican City."

I laugh without humor. "Of course."

Benedict is the only person that I count a true friend, one I can trust without question unlike recent experiences with Christian. And as far as I'm concerned, Benedict is my *only* brother. If I ever were to cross paths with Damien again, I know Benedict would pass me the knife to gut him.

One happy family.

Looks like I'm not going to be able to get any advice tonight. The only thing I can do is pop an Ambien and hope for a dreamless sleep.

Because tomorrow morning, I'll be facing Kate Winter again. And this time she won't be spreading her legs and offering me a sample of her nectar. She'll be presenting me with a dossier of potential wives.

Kate

It's déjà vu the next morning when I look out my apartment window to find X and the Rolls-Royce waiting against the curb. Maddie peers over my shoulder.

"I still don't get it," she says, and I can hear the disappointment lacing her tone. "Why did they specifically ask for you rather than me? It's *my* agency, after all."

Now that the contract has been signed, I can tell my sister everything. Which is good because that whole secrecy thing won't fly when I'm getting picked up by a Rolls with a license plate that reads *Royal*. Besides,

I'd accepted the job—after the king and queen agreed to double my fee for working with such a reluctant client. Well, it was the queen's suggestion. Turns out that despite the business being Maddie's baby, my recent success at facilitating what I thought had been a few discreet celebrity matches had not flown under the radar of the royal family.

"Come on, Mads," I say. "It's a gold star for the business regardless of whether it's you or me facilitating the matches. Plus, you're my partner in crime, so it's not like we can't work on Nikolai's profile together." In fact, the only thing I cannot disclose to anyone other than Maddie is the list of potential candidates.

She is obviously still pouting, but as much as I love my big sister and her flair for business, I am the one with the perfect match record—fifteen happy couples in just the past six months alone. It's all in the interviews. One face-to-face conversation with each potential partner—separately, of course—and I can either feel their chemistry…or not. That, coupled with my limited celebrity experience, I'm sure is why they asked for me, but I don't rub it in. While I'm proud I've taken so well to the business these past two years, what does it say that I can find happy endings for everyone—except myself?

Then I'm reminded that I risked my heart once, and the payoff was total devastation. No, thank you. I'm good with focusing on everything and anything other than that.

I wave to X and hold up a finger, letting him know I'll be right there. Then I turn to face my sister, staring into icy blue eyes that mirror my own.

"Remember, Maddie, we need this fee. We are almost due for another quarterly payment at Silver Maples." Gran's been deteriorating, her Alzheimer's getting worse almost by the week. We're her sole financial support. Actually, we're her sole *everything*. As much as it kills us not to have her at home, caring for her like she did raising us, her condition has declined too much. Silver Maples is a top-rated facility, one of the best in Europe. And it's priced accordingly. It's just out of our financial means at the moment, but I intend to change that.

I don't mention the part about receiving *no* fee at all if I don't get Nikolai down the aisle—if he is my first and *only* fail. I also may have omitted that despite my vow to find him a suitable queen, I already know what it feels like for his stubble to chafe my thighs, for his tongue to swirl around my swollen clit. Or to know that despite the matches that are perfect for Nikolai Lorentz on paper, the only chemistry I'm sure of at this point is whatever happened in that garden maze between myself and our future king.

"Shit," I mutter under my breath and slip past her. I need to stop thinking myself into climax before I've even had my first sip of espresso. "I'm late." I grab my dossier off our small kitchen table and reach for the small cup that should have three shots of my morning wake-up medicine when I realize the espresso machine is unplugged. I never forget my morning shot. Ugh. I am way off my game, which is not an auspicious beginning to day one with my most important client. *"Shit,"* I say louder and then groan my acceptance at another morning with an empty belly. I kiss my sister on the cheek. "Love you!" And then I dart out the door before she has a chance to respond.

Not that I'm expecting a repeat performance of what happened yesterday, but I wear my auburn waves loose today—in case of any mishaps. Better to have my hair down and unfettered than to attempt the whole conservative look only to wind up disheveled and unkempt. Because I much prefer *kempt*.

X holds open the car door, and I enter to find a veritable feast waiting for me on a small table attached to the wall that separates the rear of the vehicle from the front. There's a bowl of the reddest strawberries I've ever seen, a small basket of scones and a stainless-steel travel mug of what I assume is coffee.

My eyes widen as I lower myself into my seat, and I glance at X before he closes the door. He offers me a small bow, and I blush, embarrassed at the royal treatment when my upbringing is probably more common than he can imagine.

"Compliments of His Royal Highness, Prince Nikolai."

While I'm sure my fresh breakfast probably cost him no more than a few seconds of his time, a quick royal order via text, I can't fight the warmth spreading through my veins that he thought of me at all.

"Thank you, X," I say with a smile I'm unable to suppress, and he nods before closing the door.

I settle into the plush leather of my seat, pulling a napkin that's folded in the shape of a swan from the table before me. A pang of guilt rests in my chest for whoever created this small masterpiece only to have me stain it with berry juice or dripped coffee. Yet I shake it out, a swan no more, and lay it across my lap as X pulls smoothly from the curb.

I opted for pants today—a cropped black pair with

a green silk blouse. And flats. I'd pretty much taken every precaution to avoid a repeat performance with the prince, and I smile smugly to myself at how easy it will be to keep my panties on today.

I unlock the lid to the mug and breathe in the rich aroma, biting back a moan as I do. Whatever brand of coffee is in there, it's miles above the quality of the espresso I buy on sale at the corner market.

I knock on the window that separates me from X, and instead of him lowering it, his voice pipes through a speaker to my left.

"Can I help you, Miss Kate?"

I roll my eyes at his insistence on formality but decide not to give him a hard time.

"It's kind of lonely here," I tell him. "Can we talk without the intercom?"

I hear him clear his throat. "As you wish, Miss Kate."

The window lowers, and I pop a strawberry into my mouth before leaning toward the open space between us. But the expanse is too wide for my torso, and I end up falling to my knees, a dribble of berry juice on my chin. I wipe it clean and scoot the rest of the way to the window frame, leaning through it so X's strong profile is in view.

"Did you make the swan?" I ask.

His eyes remain on the road as he replies. "No, Miss."

"Did you make the coffee?"

"No, Miss."

"Would you like a strawberry?"

At this I see the faintest tug on the corner of his mouth, and I decide that along with making sure I send

Nikolai Lorentz down the aisle, I'm going to make X smile.

"No, Miss," he says, and my shoulders sag.

I follow his eyes to the road ahead and realize we're not headed in the direction of the palace. For a second my heart stutters in my chest.

"Okay, you're not going to ply me with strawberries and scones only to dump me in the river with a backpack full of stones, right?"

Again that twitch of his lip, but it doesn't go beyond that.

"We *are* heading to the river," he says. "But His Highness said nothing about a backpack."

I narrow my eyes even though he won't look in my direction. Despite heading toward the body of water I've avoided most of my living years, I decide to trust my life is not in danger and slide back to my seat, this time bringing a warm blueberry scone with me. Seriously? How is it still warm?

Just as I relax and bring the pastry to my lips, we roll to a stop. X, however, does not leave his seat. Before I can ask him if we've reached our destination, my door opens, and I see the prince—not in a rumpled dress shirt and tuxedo pants but in a fitted black T-shirt and dark washed jeans. I know what I said about not being a preteen fangirl, but holy hell. This man in the flesh is a vision to behold.

He extends his arms wide as if he's brought the world to my doorstep, and based on the breakfast alone, it feels like he has.

"We can't possibly be expected to work indoors on a day like today," he says, his gray eyes shimmering silver in the sun.

He offers me a hand, and I take it, grabbing the dossier with my other as he pulls me into the fresh morning air.

"No," I say, trying to convince myself that the smoldering heat in my core is from the coffee I leave behind in the car. "I guess we can't."

CHAPTER FIVE

Nikolai

"THANKS FOR BREAKFAST." Kate regards me uncertainly.

"Seems only fair, Miss Winter. Especially after the delicious feast you offered me yesterday." Here's hoping that my wolfish smile covers any sincerity that might poke through my veneer. "Nice pants, by the way." They fit slim against her shape, hugging the soft swell of her thighs, tapering at her small waist. I take my time drinking her in for two reasons. One: she looks even better than she did in my dreams last night. Two: it's time to scare her off.

I don't care a whit about ancient marriage requirements. But my father is the king, and Edenvale is a strict monarchy. No constitution. No parliament. His word is absolute law.

But despite his decree, I cannot marry. I *will* not. My heart hasn't been whole for years. To subject a woman to a lifetime of darkness—to a love I cannot give—is anything but fair. I may not play by the rules in my day-to-day—or night-by-night—affairs, but I am straightforward. Each beauty I bed knows full well

I have nothing to offer the morning after other than burying my cock in her one more time.

I do like a proper goodbye, after all.

And I also like to be clear that I will not share my future crown.

Father has to be bluffing about this twenty-ninth birthday bullshit. He can't take the throne from me. He wouldn't. What are his other options? Benedict would yield our sovereign power to the Roman Pope. Damien? My cousin Ingrid, who is still a child? Nightgardin would be licking its chops if that happened.

A hot copper taste fills my mouth. The inside of my cheek hurts from the involuntary bite.

Damien destroyed my world. His scandal nearly brought down our entire lineage. Now he is banished. Not even allowed to claim Edenvale citizenship. No, that bottom-feeder will never be permitted to call himself more than "King of Traitors."

Father has no other choice, if he wants to avoid passing the crown from his bloodline. He will have to relent, to compromise, come around and see things from my point of view. It is that or let the kingdom fall to ruin, and that—he knows—is not an option.

My shoulders relax. I'll indulge in Miss Winter's little game for the time being, but she doesn't know that I'm the one writing the rules, and that I only play to win.

"Ahem, Highness?" Her exaggerated throat clearing breaks my thoughts. "My eyes are up here."

I allow my gaze to slowly rake over the swell of her perfect breasts. "I know exactly where your eyes are, Miss Winter, and might I say that's a fetching color of shadow. Makes your eyes appear deeper than the Bottomless Lake."

Kate sucks in a ragged breath, one evidenced by the rapid rise and fall of her chest rather than heard.

"Can we get down to business?" Pleading fills her voice.

"That all depends. Would getting down to...*business* bring you pleasure?" I dribble innuendo over every sentence. My mask is perfect. I'm every inch the rakish rogue everyone has come to expect. Kate Winter has no idea that my heart accelerates in her vicinity, kicks into fifth faster than my Ferrari 250 Testa Rossa.

And she never will.

She balls her free hand into a fist while the other clutches a portfolio, her fingertips white from her grip. Bet Little Miss Ice Queen would love nothing better than landing a punch right in my arrogant smirk. She can take a number. There are many in the line before her.

Plus she's safer wanting nothing more to do with me than our business dealings.

"X," I call, not breaking my gaze. "The poles."

"Very good, Highness." He clicks his heels and strides to the trunk of the Rolls. Good old X. Familiar as my shadow.

"I'm not really a nature girl." She casts a baleful look at the long grass, swatting away a hovering insect. "But I am excited to get to work. Here is the dossier." She brandishes the portfolio. "I spent last night reviewing suitable prospects and have winnowed your choices to five viable candidates." She clears her throat. "Your parents offered some input as well, wishing the choice to be someone who would buoy your image and thereby the image of the throne. Your stepmother in particular took a keen interest. The queen is a woman of many opinions."

I arch a brow. My hag of a stepmother has many feelings about my existence, none of them good. "I thought we were to do some sort of personality profile."

She breaks eye contact. "Your stepmother didn't think it was necessary to invest too much in compatibility since—well—since you don't intend this to be much of an emotional connection. You've made that point crystal clear. So I've been instructed to provide you with *appropriate* choices."

"Fascinating." A cold front blows over my chest, transforming my tone to sheer ice. I spent last night milking my cock, dreaming of her sweet, soaked pussy, and all the while she'd been reviewing *appropriate* brides. Not once in five years have I given a single fuck what a woman thinks about after I've been with her.

Not once until today.

How much is Father paying her for this trouble? My stepmother would bankrupt the royal coffers if it meant having her revenge. She won't play me the fool the way her daughter did. Victoria made me believe that a kiss meant love, not a fast track to sink her claws into my wealth—or my future throne.

These days the only crown jewels I'm prepared to offer the opposite sex rest between my legs. It's likely she is conspiring with my stepmother. No doubt yesterday's unexpected encounter was part of her carefully constructed ruse designed to disarm me. Being heir to the Edenvale throne means living with an invisible target on my back. The thing is, though, that I already know there's a sniper in my midst, and she sleeps in my father's bed.

My smile is as cool as her name. If Kate Winter hopes to lie in wait to stab a proverbial blade between my shoulder blades, then I hope she has the patience of a saint, because I aim to give her no such satisfaction.

X returns, and her expression morphs from confused to horrified.

"Fishing poles?" She gasps. "Is this your idea of a joke?"

"Fishing is one of my many hobbies," I lie smoothly. "And it seems an apt metaphor given our current situation." I take a pole from X and hand it to her.

She grips it without complaint, understanding the gesture isn't a request, but an order from her prince.

I grab the dossier from her other hand, not bothering to look inside, and hand it to X. "We won't be needing that just yet," I say, then turn my attention to Kate. "After all, there are many fish in the sea, correct? Or should I say…river?" I pivot and stride toward the old Roman bridge. "And how can I be sure of your skills in catching one for me until I see you in action?"

Kate

It's a stone bridge, I remind myself. A sturdy, stone, won't-crumble-beneath-your-feet bridge. There's no need to tell him I can't swim.

Though the swelling in my ankle has gone down, the lingering ache still slows my gait. He walks a few paces ahead of me, not bothering to wait. Decidedly different behavior from yesterday when he carried me after my fall—saw to it that I made it home safe. Hell, he even sent me breakfast this morning. I knew I was stupid to think it meant anything more than feeding the help, that Nikolai Lorentz was anything other than what the media portrayed.

I catch up to him at the center of the bridge where nothing else waits for us other than two buckets, one of which must be bait, the other to hold what we catch. I swallow hard when I note the height—or lack thereof—of the stone wall separating us from the river below. Nikolai perches casually on the low barrier, reaches into the bucket and pulls from it what looks like a small slice of sausage.

"What is that?" I ask, wrinkling my nose.

He shrugs. "X prepared it. Says it's his best recipe for catching trout. You met Beatrice in the kitchen yesterday, yes? Our head cook? Tonight's royal meal depends on what you catch for us today."

His tone is more cold than playful, yet I decide to humor him.

"Well, then," I say. "I've got plenty of suggestions for takeout when this goes *royally* amiss."

He buries the hint of a smile, but I see it nonetheless and take it as a sign that I do have the power to break through whatever wall he's hiding behind today. I remind myself that my livelihood depends on it and let out a breath before reaching into the small bucket and pinching a slimy piece of bait between my thumb and forefinger.

I shudder at the feel of the foreign substance against my skin but do not dare complain. I watch as Nikolai fixes his bait to his hook and mimic his movements precisely. Maybe this won't be so difficult after all.

He raises a brow. "You've fished before?"

I shake my head. "I'm a quick learner," I say, realizing I've nowhere to wipe my hand and opt for the ledge of the wall I don't dare sit on myself.

He casts his line into the river, and again I follow suit.

Piece of disgusting, slimy cake.

He finally grins. "May the best fisherman win," he says. "Not that it's a competition."

I smile. "You're on, Your Highness."

We fish in silence, him still sitting on the wall while I stand a pace behind it. In less than three minutes his line tugs at the pole, and Nikolai whoops in response, standing to reel in his catch.

I can't help but marvel at the ease of his movements, the flex of his biceps as he rotates the crank on the pole. And it's this lapse in my attention, this gravitational pull he seems to have on me despite every bit of logic saying it shouldn't, that causes the tug on my own line to catch me off guard.

My body yanks forward, and I stumble. It all happens in the space of a few seconds. I don't even have time to scream before I knock into the wall and pitch right over it.

The water is cool, yet it burns my lungs and throat as I panic and breathe it in. I cough, but it only makes me take in more water. In this strange, suspended panic, I note the clarity of the river, that I can see through the surface and to the bridge to where it looks like something is falling toward me as I sink.

As quickly as I was yanked off the bridge, strong hands wrap around me and tug me toward the surface. When I break through, I cough up the water I couldn't release seconds ago and gasp for air. Instinct has me thrashing in his arms, but he doesn't let go.

"Kate!" he yells, his voice hoarse. "Christ, Kate! Stop fighting me and put your feet down. It's only five feet deep!"

His words register, and I cease movement, letting my legs straighten below me while I still cling to his arm with my own.

My shoes touch the riverbed, and I stand on my tiptoes, my five-foot-five height keeping my face well above water.

We reach the bank, and I collapse onto my ass, humiliation seeping in as I cough up another mouthful of water.

Nikolai falls onto his back, panting, his T-shirt and jeans plastered to his muscled frame.

"Christ almighty," he says, catching his breath. "Why didn't you tell me you couldn't swim?"

I try to convince myself that this job is worth it, that no matter what other disasters befall throughout the length of this contract, it will be worth it in the end. Because if I fail, it's Maddie and Gran who will pay the price.

"You're my prince," I say dully. "You said we were fishing, so I obeyed."

He bolts upright, brows pulled together. "Is that really—?" he sputters. "You think I would endanger—?" But he trails off again. He reaches for my face, resting a palm gingerly against my cheek, and it's almost as hard to breathe as being underwater. "Are you okay?"

Genuine concern laces his words. This is a Nikolai I've never seen in the pages of a magazine. This man did not exist in the maze yesterday.

"Yes," I whisper, the heat in his palm making me forget I'm soaking wet.

"I told you," he says, his gray eyes darkening to black, "I will not marry."

I nod slowly. "And your father will keep the throne from you if you do not. Nikolai, when you stormed out yesterday, he mentioned Damien…"

A soft, guttural sound emanates from his throat.

"If you want the throne," I continue, "then finding a bride is the only way." And the only way to keep my grandmother getting the best care that our country has to offer. But I don't tell him that. As much as I am drawn to him, I can't get close to another man. Especially not another bad boy who doesn't seem to care about anything other than his next thrill. My heart can only take so much.

He lets out a long breath. "So it is," he says, and my heart tightens at the sound of defeat in those words. "Then we find someone who will play by my rules, who knows she is queen in name only, and that I will govern Edenvale as I see fit when it's my time."

I nod again. "If that is your choice."

He lets out a bitter laugh. "Choice," he says through gritted teeth. "Wouldn't that be a luxury?"

I shiver, the cold setting in and seeping into my bones. He drops his hand to my neck, my collarbone and then to breast, my nipple hard against the cold, wet fabric of my blouse, a trail of heat in its wake.

"What if I choose to touch you like this?" he asks, his lips a fraction of an inch from mine. "Would you choose that, too?" He glances toward the river. Then his gaze burns into mine again. "Because you *have* a choice, Kate. You should have told me that you live along a river yet have never bathed in it."

I feel the prick of tears and try to will them away.

"Maddie and I—my sister—lost our parents when they drove off the road that winds along the mountain's edge. The river was deeper than five feet where their car plunged in." A single tear escapes, and he brushes it away, the gesture too sweet. Too intimate. "I was too young to remember them but not too young to develop a fear of the water. The funny thing is, Maddie says I was an excellent swimmer from a young age, but it's like my mind has blocked that part out. So...here we are."

He runs a hand through his soaked black hair. "You should have told me," he says again, and I startle to see the intensity in his eyes. "*You* have choice, Kate. With me. Nothing is an order. Do you understand that?"

"Yes," I whisper.

He places a hand behind my neck and lowers me to the ground, my body a willing accomplice.

"You will find me a royal bride," he says, hovering over me. A bead of water drips off his skin and splashes near the corner of my lips. It takes all my self-restraint not to lick it.

"Yes."

"I will not love her," he adds.

"I know," I whisper.

"I *cannot* love anyone." His voice is a low vibration, one I feel in his chest against mine.

"I know," I say again, cursing the beating of my heart that seems to speed up the nearer he gets. We might be from two different worlds, but we have that much in common. I *can* love, but I won't. Not when I've known so much loss.

"But I want you," he says, his breath warm against my lips.

"I want you, too," I admit.

He flicks out his tongue, running it along my bottom lip, and I grind my pelvis into his.

"Do you *choose* this, Kate? Do you choose what I'm offering?"

My body has already complied. All that's left is my voice.

"I do, Your Highness."

"Call me Nikolai."

I let out a trembling breath. "I do—Nikolai." His name tastes as delicious as his hungry mouth.

He kisses me, long and slow and deep until my toes curl and my core is on fire.

"Say my name again," he growls, his erection firm against my aching clit.

"Nikolai," I whisper, and his tongue plunges into my mouth again.

I may have the freedom of choice, but I also have the wisdom to know this is a foolish one to make. I'll have to add a note in my planner to regret this sometime tomorrow.

CHAPTER SIX

Nikolai

I BURY MY fingers into her thick coil of auburn hair and pull, not hard, but enough to deepen our kiss. Kate's tears place me on unfamiliar ground. The story of her loss threatens to undo my expertly built defenses. I don't know how to tell her this, but in some ways, I understand her pain. Once upon a time, many years ago, a car accident changed my own world. She and I share an unexpected connection, both forever marked by a tragedy that changed the course of our lives.

Damn it. My pulse thunders in my ears. I don't want to be curious about Kate, to be interested in her as a *person* and not another notch in my belt. I channel my frustration into tangling my tongue with hers, demanding more, demanding everything, and she moans into my open mouth, offering herself freely.

My chest tightens like a vise. I gasp a mumbled curse. This kiss is taking over, filling my veins, replacing the blood. *Slow the fuck down. Keep it physical.* Remember that's my MO—making women cry out my name and wanting nothing more in return than my own physical release. I reach down to circle my thumbs over her peaked nipples, hard nubs against her wet, silky top. She moans again. Louder.

I tear away, one foot in heaven and one in hell. It's time to get a grip, to calm myself and focus. After all, getting a woman off is what I do best. My uncertainty fades as I take charge, increasing the pressure. Not much, just enough to turn that moan into a gasp, followed by a soft squeak. I break our kiss and nip her plump lower lip, tasting the hint of cherry lip balm. Then I continue my leisurely torment down her jaw to the sensitive place on her neck, relishing her rapid pulse and trace of perfume that wasn't washed away in the river. Chanel No. 5.

She is killing me in the best of ways.

"God, you smell brilliant." I give her a soft bite. Not enough to leave a mark, but enough that I've got her full attention. She moans. All women enjoy a little domination in the bedroom. "Like that?"

"Mmmmm," she purrs.

I bite again, wiping away the sting with the flat of my tongue. "I asked you a question. I am your prince. I expect you to respond." My tone is authoritative, yet teasing. I want control, but I also want her to know she's safe—safe from the river, from the painful memories she buries. I'll erase it all with a swipe of my tongue. Another nip of teeth.

She presses her hips against me. "Feels so good," she murmurs. "If X wasn't close, I'd be on my knees filling my mouth with your cock."

So my prim-and-proper ice queen likes to talk dirty. Blood sings through my veins, a pounding chorus, as I thicken in an instant. "Good thing X took a drive."

She stills. "He's gone?"

"I heard him leave while we walked toward the bridge."

She frowns. "He knew you'd seduce me?"

I shrug. "Maybe he wanted a croissant?"

She slides away. My body aches at the gap, and for a moment, I falter. Who is really in control here?

"You seduce many women, don't you, Sire?"

No point lying. *"Nikolai,"* I remind her, my voice firm. I want my name dripping off her lips in a torrent of pleasure. "Call me by my name." Might as well admit there is more to wanting to hear her say it than a simple, sexual ego booster. Every cell in my being craves her closer, wanting to rub against her and smooth away my ragged edges, to see if she is the one who possesses whatever the fuck I need to be made whole.

Good God. I'm pussy drunk.

"You seduce many women, don't you, *Nikolai*?" She bites her bottom lip, and my cock strains against my jeans, but I force my voice to remain steady.

"Yes," I say simply. I'm Mr. Right Now. Not Mr. Right.

"A bad boy."

I crook my lips into an arrogant smile, the mask that she expects her future ruler to wear. I have a rakehell reputation to uphold. "That seems to be the general opinion."

She shakes her head. "Why not give in?" she murmurs, more to herself than me. "Live dangerously for once in my life." She refocuses her gaze on me. "We can do whatever it is we are about to do and still remain professional."

My brows rise. "Your mouth sheathing my cock is

professional?" I swallow hard, and she notices, grinning, no doubt, at the effect she has on me.

She narrows her gaze as if to size me up. "Yes. Once I know what you like, I'll be that much better positioned to find it for you."

"I can think of many positions I'd like to find you in."

She purses her lips. Then a flicker of uncertainty passes over her face. "Tell me how you like it."

"Pardon?" My own eyes widen. "How I like getting sucked off?" She wants a lesson?

"Yes, tell me in thorough detail. If you teach me well, perhaps you'll get a handsome reward." She palms me over the wet denim of my jeans. "I'm a quick study and also quite good at taking direction."

I decide right then and there that despite what she's been hired to do—and how much I detest the thought of finding a bride—I love being around this most surprising woman.

Wait…love? The word doesn't belong anywhere in my vocabulary. This is no good. My heart better go sit its ass in a corner. I clear my throat. "You want to know how to suck a dick? Very well. First, the woman in question needs to crave it. I want her to approach my cock like it's a chocolate fucking fudge sundae and she hasn't eaten in a week."

Her lids flutter. "Go on."

Shit. I can talk dirty in five languages, but I've never given an explicit lesson in the art of performing a blow job. And believe me—it is a goddamn art. "I need some encouragement," I tell her, my voice growing hoarse with need. "A little inspiration."

She arches a brow. "And how can I do that?"

I pretend to think it over. "Are you wearing a matching set?"

She nods with a shy smile. "I do own the bra to match my pink lace panties," she says, then licks her lips. "But I didn't wear it today."

My throat thickens. And if it's at all possible, my cock grows even harder, and I want nothing more than for her to rip my jeans from my legs. *Mission accomplished, Miss Winter.* The image of what lies beneath her drenched clothing will inspire me for days and nights to come.

What can I say? Kate Winter is my fucking muse. Literally.

"Shall we continue with the lesson?" I ask.

"Please," she says. "It's been a while since—well, I think I mentioned yesterday that it's been a while. Period."

I bury the surge of jealousy at the thought of her mouth on any other man and decide to give her exactly what she's asking for—so that she may give it to me.

"Outside of a sixty-nine, I prefer to stand," I tell her, already imagining her kneeling before me. "Gives me good control and a great view. Hands are important. Use them. I love a mouth on me, but touch is a must. Stroke my shaft. Massage my sac. Gradually increase the tempo. That's when I'll need some tongue on the tip, swirling and sucking like I'm your favorite flavor of Popsicle."

She rolls her eyes. "Cool it with the food references. You're making me hungry." Her tone is teasing, but I can tell from the way her pupils dilate that she is soaked.

"Never use your teeth. Simply lick and swirl until you're ready."

"For what?" She sounds drugged.

"To take me as deep as you can go. A gentleman never crams his cock into a lady's throat. He waits, patiently, but what he wants is for her to suck him down. And all the while, hold eye contact. Trust me on this. A guy loves it when you take it all and let him see how much you love every inch."

She runs a hand over her hair. "And for the end?"

"Swallow," I say bluntly and shrug. She asked, so I might as well give her the truth.

"I've never done that," she whispers. "I've always been too intimidated."

"Well, you don't have to," I tell her quickly. Again it comes, that inexplicable need to make her feel safe. "It's just…you asked what's the best. That is the best, Pet. Nothing like it."

She stays quiet for a long moment. Long enough that I start to wonder if I've pissed her off—or even worse, scared her from even wanting to try.

"Stand, Sire," she finally says, and I obey without question. She stands too, stepping forward to close the narrow distance between us, all the while keeping her gaze locked to my face.

Then she sinks to her goddamn knees.

"I've never mixed business and pleasure." She reaches to undo my fly. "But this is my most important job yet, so perhaps I should ensure you get the royal treatment."

My hands fist in her hair, and I know from the determined look in her eyes that I'm about to be destroyed.

Kate

His jeans are snug against his hard, muscled thighs, and despite them being soaked in the river, it only takes me seconds to pull them to his ankles.

My nipples peak against my cold, wet top, and I wonder if he knows how close to the edge I already am. Just from his words. It was never like this with Jean-Luc, and as soon as the thought enters my mind, I'm awash in a wave of guilt. How dare I compare what I'm about to do to a man I met yesterday to a man I'd planned to be with for the rest of my life?

And yet it's the truth.

I loved my fiancé, but I can't recall wanting him with this sort of hunger. I'd always felt performing oral sex to be more of an obligation than anything else. And he had always finished so quickly that I never knew what he really liked.

But I *want* to taste Nikolai so badly that my pulse throbs between my legs.

I start by placing a soft kiss on his inner thigh, then shift my heavy gaze to his.

"More," he says, and my core tightens at the command.

I kiss his other thigh, this time a little higher up, and I have to grab his backside to steady myself.

He lets out a groan.

"Hands," he says, his voice tight, and I do believe I've made it difficult for my prince to speak.

I look up at him and grin, releasing his ass with my right hand so I can cup his balls. Then, without warning, I swirl my tongue over his tip, the precum salty on my taste buds. We both moan.

His hands tug at my hair, and I move my own to join my mouth, taking him deeper as he slides slick through my palm.

"Fuck," he hisses. *"Yes*, Pet. More. Goddamn, I need more."

My clit swells at the sound of his need, a delicious, aching pulse between my thighs, and I can't hold back a whimper as he sinks deeper into my mouth, as I let the taste of him fill me.

Deeper and faster, my hand grips his throbbing shaft, and I feel his thighs begin to shake. I hold his gaze as I bury him to the hilt, and for the brief moment when he begins to teeter over the edge, I see past the facade to a brokenness that draws me further into his orbit.

He shudders and growls. I swallow his release, an intimate connection I never knew was possible. I back away, ready to force my trembling limbs to stand, but he collapses to his knees in front of me.

His hands cup my cheeks, and he stares into my eyes. Without a word he kisses me so hard and deep I can barely catch my breath. He lowers me to the ground, wordless still, his lips never leaving mine. His hand slides beneath my blouse, and I buck against him as he pinches my sensitive peak.

We are animals, communicating with nothing other than our shared savage need, and I *need* this. I *need* his hands on me, in me—I need Nikolai Lorentz everywhere. And because we speak the same language, he knows, and I find him wrenching my pants from my hips, down to my knees, all the while his tongue tangling with mine.

Finally, when two fingers plunge inside me, immediately hitting the right spot, I call out his name in an overwhelming torrent of sensation.

"Nikolai!"

And then I finally close my eyes and see nothing but stars.

I'm nothing short of a mess when we make our way to the road and find X waiting outside the Rolls. Nikolai, despite his dip in the river as well, looks nothing short of spectacular. Or maybe that's all I can see after what he's done to me.

What *has* he done? I feel satiated yet hungry. Remade but ruined.

X opens the door as we approach, not once letting his impassive gaze give away that he knew Nikolai had planned to seduce me. But when I look inside the car and see my scones and fruit replaced by a small platter of croissants, I can't help but burst into a fit of laughter.

Nikolai's brows pull together, and it takes every ounce of control for me to simply motion toward the open door and say, *"Look."*

He does, and as soon as he sees the pastries, he's laughing too, and I am surprised the way my heart surges to hear such a sound—a genuine emotion from Prince Nikolai, and I get to bear witness.

X clears his throat and raises a brow.

"Your Highness. Miss Winter—I thought you might have worked up an appetite."

I decide not to deny it because damn—I *am* starving. So I reach inside the car and grab a chocolate croissant, tearing off a piece and shoving it into a surprised Nikolai's mouth before tearing into the rest of it with my teeth.

"You're right," I say, mouth full, hair tangled and probably full of sand, clothes still wet and plastered to my body. "I'm famished."

X nods. "Your Highness, I take it there are supplies to collect from the bridge?"

Nikolai swallows his bite of croissant. "Yes, thank you. One fishing pole, the bucket of bait and Miss Winter's dossier. You can throw the trout I caught back into the river."

"Yes, Your Highness," he says, not questioning why we are short one fishing pole.

Once X is out of earshot, I point at Nikolai with my half-eaten croissant.

"Hey, I thought you said tonight's royal meal depended on what I caught on our little fishing expedition."

He shrugs and gives me a sheepish grin, another expression I don't expect, and it disarms me completely.

"I despise seafood, actually," he says. "But I was hoping to enjoy putting you through the wringer."

I open my mouth at an attempt to unleash my fury on him, but he silences me with a kiss, and I'm caught so off guard that I simply melt into it.

"How about a truce?" he says against me, and I squeak out my answer, the momentary fury dissolving into dust.

"Okay," I whisper.

"Okay," he says.

"But this *cannot* happen again, Your Highness. We have— I mean *I* have a job to do."

He nods. "Of course. Never again, Miss Winter. You have my word."

I sigh. I know he's soon to be my king, that my job

is to find him a queen, but right now I don't believe his word for one tiny second. And that impish grin on his face tells me that neither does he.

CHAPTER SEVEN

Nikolai

"MY, MY, ISN'T His Highness in quite the chipper mood?" My wicked stepmother, Queen Adele, sizes me up from across the mahogany table. Even when it is just she, my father and I in residence at the palace, she insists on using the formal dining room that can accommodate up to fifty guests. Overhead hang three large crystal chandeliers, and lining the wood-paneled room are suits of armor interspersed with the images of frowning black-haired men, my ancestors, the kings of old.

From the looks of their faces, dark and brooding is a family tradition.

"As a matter of fact, *Majesty*, I *am* in good spirits." I wipe my lips with a linen napkin before crooking them into a smile as fake as her own. The queen's gaze narrows as she tries to see through my mocking mask.

Lots of luck, love.

My father cuts his roast, oblivious as always to the private war that I carry out with the hag. "I understand you met with the matchmaker this afternoon.

She seems a competent woman." He spears the beef with his fork. "Most enthusiastic."

"Quite." An image of Kate Winter flashes, one where she is on her knees, hair wet and wild, sucking my cock like some sort of mythic water goddess, and I suppress a satisfied grin.

"Rather common, if you ask me." My stepmother gives an audible sniff.

"Good thing no one did," I growl, my mouth flat-lining.

She ignores the warning in my voice. "I do admit to having second thoughts on Miss Winter. After all, how can a commoner have the proper breeding necessary to discern fine taste? Edenvale *is* the second-oldest throne in all of Europe. The realm expects certain standards."

White-hot fury builds behind my eyes. This snobby shrew isn't fit to lick the sole of one of Kate's heels, let alone dare to speak her name with such disdain. True, my favorite matchmaker isn't blue-blooded, but she has more natural grace and elegance in one of her little fingers than Adele has in her entire Botoxed body.

Who knows what prompted Father to marry her? I barely remember my real mother, but from all accounts, it was a love match. Queen Cordelia remains well-beloved by her people to this day, no thanks to Adele, who likes to pretend she never existed.

I study the fine lines that groove my stepmother's frown. She has always been a sourpuss, but since her only daughter Victoria's death she's turned downright wicked.

The last vestiges of my good mood vanish. When Adele married my lonely father the only bright spot to the arrangement came in the form of her beautiful and vivacious nineteen-year-old daughter, my stepsister and first love. I was a foolish twenty-three-year-old boy determined to make Victoria my queen. While Father disapproved of the relationship, Adele could not hide her ambition. She might not have liked the idea of me making love to her daughter but persuaded Father to allow the engagement to proceed because it would make Victoria a queen. She even argued that it would strengthen Edenvale's royal ties to have not one but two generations of our royal bloodlines matched. Their aristocratic family has always been one of the wealthiest and most influential in our kingdom. But they've always had a reputation for being ambitious.

Too ambitious for my liking.

Over the years, whenever I indulged in a whiskey too many and allowed my thoughts to wander, it had seemed conceivable that Adele might have masterminded the whole affair, put her only child in my path, advising her on how to best seduce her way into a lonely prince's heart. If Victoria had survived the accident, perhaps she'd have grown to be as calculating and bloodless as the woman sneering down her aristocratic nose at me. The question, though, will never be answered. My youngest brother, Damien, saw to that, ending her life with his usual recklessness, earning his banishment and my everlasting hatred.

"Well, do try to retain your good mood for Saturday evening," Adele says, dipping her spoon into the lobster bisque.

"What's Saturday?" I crook my finger, signaling the butler to bring me more wine. I am tempted to grab the whole damn bottle, get too drunk to dream. I don't want nightmares of Victoria disturbing my sleep tonight.

"Didn't Miss Winter tell you?" My stepmother's lifeless smile is stiff and doesn't reach her cruel eyes. "She has arranged your first date."

Kate

"No," I say, when I open my apartment door to find X standing there. "Absolutely not." Before I can close the door in the man's face—and I would feel horrid doing so, but this crosses the line—Maddie sidles up behind me.

"Who's your friend?" she asks, though I'm sure she can tell by his immaculate suit that he is not one who dwells on Market Street. I glance at my own attire, a freaking Fall Out Boy T-shirt and skinny jeans. I look like an American teenager.

"Maddie, this is X. He works for the royal family."

My sister pulls the door the rest of the way open. She, of course, is in a perfectly beautiful sundress, because *she* has a date. Which is fine because I was very much looking forward to Netflix, and ice cream, and not thinking about the strange events that have transpired this week. But no, the prince has to butt into my plans, my thoughts, my whatever—simply because he can.

X offers my sister a slight bow, and she backhands me on the shoulder.

"*This* is the prince's driver—the guy who picked you up the other morning? You didn't say he was a silver fox!" she whisper-shouts, but the man is standing right in front of us.

X's brows rise, the slightest hint of his amusement.

"Miss Kate," he says. "His Highness says it is part of your professional obligation."

I roll my eyes.

"What obligation?" Maddie asks.

"Tell him *no*," I say to X, ignoring my sister.

He pulls a phone from the inside pocket of his suit jacket and glances at the screen.

"Miss Kate declines your invitation," he says, and my stomach drops. The prince has been listening to our entire interaction.

When I hear his voice, my body tingles in response, and I silently curse Nikolai Lorentz.

"Kate," he says. X points the phone toward me and my sister. "I'm going to be late for the date that *you* set up if you don't get down here in the next three minutes."

I huff out a breath and try to ignore my sister's wide eyes and mouth open in a surprised O.

"Your Highness—" I start, but he clears his throat, interrupting me.

"Nikolai," he corrects me, and I repress an exasperated scream.

"*Nikolai*. I think you are confused. This is *your* date. I set it up, but believe me when I say that both you and the Countess of Wynberry will be most put out by me joining you for dinner."

Maddie backhands me again, this time harder, but she still says nothing.

Nikolai's raucous laugh rings out from the phone in X's hand.

"You won't actually *join* us," he says. "You'll be in the car with X. Beatrice has prepared a veritable feast for you to dine on while you wait for my cue."

My fists clench at my sides, and I don't bother stifling my groan.

"You have some nerve," I say.

"I need a wingman."

"No."

"I need to be called to an urgent meeting, an out if things go south. Because if the countess doesn't go for my proposed arrangement, I promise things will go— southerly," he adds, his words laced with amusement.

"No," I maintain.

There is silence for a few long beats, and I hold my breath until he speaks again.

"If I behave *badly*," he says, slowly drawing out each word, "which I've been known to do, I could scare off a potential prospect. But if someone is there to give me a more respectable exit should I need one, well, then, we all win. Don't we?" He pauses to let his words sink in before he puts the final nail in the coffin that is my fate for this evening. "You don't want to chance me *not* making it to the altar. Do you, Kate?"

White-hot fury pulses through me. Does he know the king and queen will refuse my fee—no matter how tireless I work—if he does not marry? How dare he use such leverage against me? But because I cannot let Maddie carry our grandmother's financial burden alone, I say what I need to say to shut him up before he reveals too much.

"Fine," I relent through gritted teeth. "I'll be right down."

X sighs and ends the call as I spin into my apartment. My sister follows.

"You're accompanying *the prince* on his date. Oh. My. God, Katie. Why didn't I get this freaking job?"

I grab my bag from the foot of my bed and sling it over my shoulder. "Right now, Maddie, I wish you had."

I don't even bother looking in the mirror. I storm toward the door where X waits patiently.

"You're not even going to change?" my sister asks from behind me, and I shake my head, answering her over my shoulder.

"You heard the man. He's going to be late, and I sure as hell don't want to keep the prince and the countess waiting."

"Have fun!" she calls, unable to mask her own giddy excitement.

Not likely.

"You too!" I offer, sincerely hoping her night goes better than mine is about to.

"If you succeed then we will have clients pouring in."

I fake a smile. "Yay!" My enthusiasm rings false, but my sister doesn't notice. She is too good to speak the language of sarcasm.

Maddie deserves all the happiness and success. She built our little company from nothing, and when my life fell apart two years ago, she gave me a place to stay and a job to dive into so I wouldn't waste away in my grief.

This is why, despite his behavior, I head downstairs and out to the Rolls-Royce parked at the curb. I'm doing this for *her*. For years I've depended on my sister, and now more than ever she's depending on me. I won't mess this up. She deserves for her business to succeed, and that means lessening the burden of paying for Gran's mounting medical bills. Every day it seems a new one arrives. She tries to hide her worry from me, but I see the dark shadows under her eyes.

X opens the door for me, and I slide into the seat opposite Nikolai. I cross my arms and try to level him with my glare.

"You look—" he starts, but I cut him off.

"Don't, Nikolai. Just don't."

He raises his brows. "I was only going to say *beautiful*. You look beautiful, Kate."

Don't, I tell myself in silence. *Don't let his words have any effect on you.*

"X," he says when the man appears behind the wheel. When did he even get there? I swear he just shut my door. "Do you know what a Fall Out Boy is?"

I snort. "Tell me you're joking." Then I see it again, the ghost of a smile on X's face. We're silently sharing a joke at Nikolai's expense.

Nikolai shrugs. "I'm assuming it is some sort of popular rock band. The music I listen to does not come with a T-shirt."

I laugh again and thrust my phone through the open partition to X.

"It's my top playlist," I say. "Can you put it on?"

The man nods, and seconds later my phone is hooked up to the car's speaker system.

The tightness in my throat loosens as "Immortals" wafts from the speakers, and I'm shocked once again when Nikolai's shoulders relax, and he cocks his head to the side and smiles.

"It's no Amadeus," he says, "but I quite like it. I suppose I'm learning I like a lot of new things these days, Miss Winter."

A chill runs along my spine, but I will it away.

Do not for one second think that he is charming. You know full well that Prince Charming he is not.

But as the anger subsides I see him clearly, his jet-black hair slicked back from his face, charcoal gray suit to match his eyes, and a royal blue tie for a pop of color. He looks so—*princely.* And gorgeous. And when his smile reaches his eyes, I have to push away the surge of emotion that rises to the surface because I've suddenly lost my grip on the anger.

I shake my head and remind myself why I'm here—to make sure this date goes smoothly. To ensure that Prince Nikolai Lorentz is one step closer to marriage—and becoming my king.

"Thank you for coming," he says softly, and I force a smile.

"Of course," I say, regaining my composure. "Nikolai?"

"Kate?"

"Have you read the entire contract between Happy Endings and your family?"

He laughs. "What's to read? You were hired to find me a wife. You're finding me a wife. I'm not interested in the fine print."

I let out a breath. So he doesn't know the consequences for me—for my family—if I fail. My anger ebbs completely as I realize Nikolai's behavior this evening is simply him being Nikolai.

"Well, then," I say. "Tell me what I need to do to make this date a success."

At this, X pulls away from the curb, and we set off for Nikolai to meet his first potential match.

CHAPTER EIGHT

Nikolai

I MUST GIVE credit to Kate's skillful matchmaker profiling. The Countess of Wynberry fits my usual physical type to a T. Platinum blond hair, come-hither bedroom eyes and ripe breasts that she proudly displays in a low-cut black silk dress offset by a necklace of glittering rubies. Hell, I don't know a guy who wouldn't describe the countess as his type. She could be a sister to that American actress Scarlett Johansson.

We meet in my private room at La Coeur, a three-star Michelin restaurant set in an eighteenth-century manor. The view of the Alps through the wide windows is unparalleled, and the gorgeous woman lounging across the table looks like she'd rather take a bite out of me than the raspberry-and-chocolate confection on her gilded plate. Yet I feel nothing but faint boredom.

Dinner went well enough. The filet was perfectly cooked and the cabernet an excellent vintage. She chattered on and on about her family's approval of our union and then of all the filthy things she planned on doing to me once we left the restaurant. I should have been hard just from her depraved words. Instead all I want is to be in my Rolls beside an auburn-haired woman in jeans who makes me feel like something I haven't felt in years.

Myself.

"You don't talk much, do you?" the countess purrs, taking her time licking her spoon clean. Her bare foot caresses my shin under the table, and I curse my unresponsive cock. The countess could douse the fire inside, the embers burning for a woman who arranged this date, but she'd fail at snuffing out the blaze.

"I do if I have something to say," I answer blandly. Her dessert does look delightful. Too bad I ordered nothing to eat for our final course, just a scotch neat. She needs to stop playing seductive games and enjoy it. But then, I've made my decision, which means she won't have time to finish, so perhaps it is for the best.

She looks curious, missing the warning in my voice. "And do you have something to say?" she asks.

Enough time wasting. "I do." I crumple my napkin on my lap and get down to business.

I say what I must in short, clipped sentences. Her eyes grow slowly wider until the whites are perfectly visible around her nearly violet irises.

Within a minute she throws a glass of champagne in my face. She has more restraint than I credited her with. I expected her to last thirty seconds max.

"You are as they say." She gathers her fur stole and rises in a huff. "A twisted monster of a man."

I blow her a kiss, and she squeals with outrage before storming for the exit.

Kate arrives in less than a minute, exactly as I expected, disheveled from sprinting to my table.

"What happened?" She gasps for air. "I thought I was here to help you to *not* cause a scene!"

I wave my hand in the air. "Trust me when I tell you that what just transpired was *not* a scene. You have read the tabloids, yes? I'm capable of so much worse. Don't you think?"

She must have run the whole way and not bothered using the restaurant's elevator. Her cheeks are flushed to a rosy red, and her chest rises and falls, heaving her breasts against the thin cotton of her T-shirt. The sight captivates me more than all the silk in Spain.

"The countess left in a rage," Kate continues. "She threatened to kick X in the parking lot if he didn't get out of her way. I'm pretty sure that counts as a scene."

I chuckle at the thought of anyone accosting X. I've seen him pin a paparazzo against a wall with one hand while dismantling his camera with the other, the action as simple as flossing his teeth. I have no idea who the hell X was before he came to the palace, but one thing is for certain: he's survived worse than the Countess of Wynberry.

"We weren't a good fit," I say lazily, sitting back in my chair. "And because no photographers are allowed inside—"

Kate lets out a breathy laugh. "Oh, there were photographers outside. I can attest to that." She shakes her head. "I have to admit my surprise… On paper you and the countess were a *perfect* match." Her tone is disappointed even as the relief is plain on her face. Strange how I am in tune to the subtleties of her emotion when we've barely been acquainted for the span of a week.

"She had a hard time hearing key truths," I say.

"Truths?" She crosses her arms and lowers her chin.

A wayward auburn strand falls across her forehead. "Nikolai, what on earth did you tell that poor woman?"

Poor woman? Perhaps that was the perfect term for her. While the countess was rich in material wealth, she lacked human qualities like warmth, companionship and kindness, characteristics I can usually dismiss. But for some reason, tonight I cannot.

"Take a seat, Kate." I gesture to the chair opposite me. "I'll tell you exactly what I said *if* you allow me to feed you bite by bite."

Kate

I cross my arms. "I'm quite stuffed," I say, not daring to glance at the dessert on the table. Even out of the corner of my eye it looks heavenly. "Beatrice fed me well with yet another back-seat feast, and I will under no circumstances let you be seen in public feeding a palace employee." Never mind that we are in a private room.

He reaches over and takes a bite of the rich-looking confection, his tongue slowly stroking the spoon, and I swallow. Then I narrow my eyes at him.

"Oh, fine," he says. "Have it your way. I simply told her what we both already know, that whoever my bride will be, it will be nothing more than a business arrangement. There will be no physical obligation other than her providing me with my own heir—however long that may take. And I will be free to satisfy my needs with whomever suits my fancy. Oh, I may have also mentioned that she will under no circumstances have any say in how I rule this country."

I throw my hand over my mouth, but it doesn't stifle

my gasp. "Nikolai!" I shout, not caring that his private room is not exactly soundproof.

He shrugs. "Oh, come now," he says. "I explained she'd want for nothing—that she'd be free to dally with anyone she pleased, so long as she was discreet."

I clench my teeth. "I know you don't plan on taking your marriage seriously, but no woman deserves to be spoken to like that. You could have been more—more *delicate*, and you know it. But you care nothing for anyone other than yourself, so you did it the Nikolai way. I should have known this job would be impossible. That *you'd* be impossible. You didn't want me here to help. Did you? You wanted me here so I'd have a front-row seat to the Nikolai Lorentz show."

My cheeks burn as I bunch my fists at my sides. One minute I'm taken aback by how beautiful he is—how he can level me with his gaze. The next I am reminded all too clearly of who he is. He is my prince—and soon, my king. He has the power to behave as he does, and I am nothing more than a subject.

I push back my chair. "I'll call for a taxi," I say, trying to keep my voice even. Anger will get me nowhere. It won't get the countess the respect he should have paid her, and it certainly won't earn any for me. He owes me nothing.

He lets me get as far as the door before he speaks.

"Kate," he says, all pretense gone from his voice. "Wait." Then I hear him let out a breath. *"Please."*

I turn to face him, and he's standing, too. But I don't dare move any closer. Even across the table he feels too near now. Because if there's one word I never expected to hear directed at me from him, it is that last one. *Please.*

"What?" I ask, the fight draining from me as he holds me with his steely, intent stare.

He runs a hand through his perfectly styled hair, loosening it so he looks more as he did on the bridge—or after he'd dived into the river to save me.

"You're right," he says. "About most of it, but you're missing one important detail."

I cross my arms and raise my brows but say nothing.

"Of course I didn't need any help," he says, palms resting on his chair. "I care nothing for my reputation. I leave that to my father, my stepmother, to all those paid to give a fuck. I suppose I'll have to clean up my act a bit once I'm king, though."

He flashes that irresistible grin, but I don't let myself fall prey to it, not this time.

"I know you don't care what others think of you," I say. "But you put my reputation on the line tonight, too, Your Highness." He winces, and the sight is something so wholly unexpected, my heart tugs involuntarily. "You may have nothing to lose, but I do. My *sister* does. Her business supports our family. We have responsibilities. This whole marriage thing that you see as a joke is how we put a roof over our heads. It's how we—"

He steps around from the chair and nearer to where I stand, the movement stealing the words from my mouth. I suck in a breath as he takes a step closer and then hold it as he rests a palm on my cheek.

"I'm an ass," he says, and I nod. "One royal prick," he adds, and I don't disagree. "Perhaps I could have been more civil to the countess. But where I truly fucked up was that I wasn't thinking of how this would affect *you*."

I clear my throat. "Wh-what important detail?" I stammer. His brows pull together. "Before, you said I was missing one important detail." I can smell the sweet scotch in the warmth of his breath. I bite my lip to keep from reacting.

He rests his forehead against mine, the gesture far too intimate, and my breath hitches.

"I asked you to come tonight, Kate, because in the span of six days, I seem to have gone from wanting nothing to do with you and what you've been hired for to not wanting you out of my sight."

He braces a palm against the door behind me, and I take a step back so I'm flush against it.

"Nikolai," I whisper. "We can't." My insistence is different than the other day at the bridge. I could take his teasing—could even pretend that we might continue our encounters and leave it at just sex. But now? What he is suggesting now is beyond possibility.

"What if there was a way?" he asks, his lips dangerously close to my own. "What if I could make you truly mine?"

My throat tightens at the thought. "But I was hired to—"

"I know," he says. "And I will continue to see the women with whom you match me. I will even be civil. But I make you this promise. I'll marry none of them."

As much as the idea of him touching another woman, let alone marrying one, already hurts in a way it should not be able to, I need him to do it because my family depends on it. *Irony, you're a cruel bitch.*

"When do you need to be married by?" I'm playing with him because I already know. Maybe if I smile the pain will ebb. One can always hope.

"My twenty-ninth birthday."

"Which is…" As if the heir's birthday isn't a national holiday.

His lids narrow as he tries to figure out what game I'm playing. "Ninety days from now."

I close my eyes and take in a long breath. Then I press my palm to his chest. "I'll make you a wager."

He laughs softly. "Go on."

"I'll see you married by your birthday," I say, my fingers already itching to grab at his tie.

He surprises me with a soft kiss before he answers. "I look forward to disappointing you."

I grip his tie and pull him as close as he can get. "And what's more, I promise you will be happy with the woman." After all, I know exactly what His Highness likes. Who better to find him not just a queen but happiness as well?

I swallow the pang of regret, the one that has me wishing for what cannot be. I do not want for him a life of misery, but I cannot let my own family fall into ruin. I will succeed. For both of us.

"You'd have to be one hell of a matchmaker, sweetheart," he says.

"Trust me." I fight to keep the tremor from my voice. "I'm the best."

CHAPTER NINE

Nikolai

IT ISN'T UNTIL nightfall that I realize that Kate never laid out the terms for our wager. I sit at my baby grand piano, my fingers flying over the keys, weaving a complex, sensual sound. Don't believe classical music can be sexy? Listen to Wagner's *Tristan and Isolde* before dismissing me. Harmony and dissonance. Brutal discord only to be thwarted by soaring passion. Music pours through me as I toy over the many ways I can extract payment from the lovely Miss Winter. Such an interesting paradox that her hair holds hints of flame even as her name promises coldness. She is both fire and ice.

I picture her lips sheathing my cock, taking me down to the root on the banks of the river. There had been a promise in her eyes, a promise that she'd be mine, if I reached out and made a claim. And so I will—at least physically, but the pleasure of the flesh is as much as I can offer. And pleasure I shall give her.

If only she had royal blood…then…perhaps she could make me overcome my vow.

"Who is the lucky lady?" a deep voice says behind me, and I strike a wrong key.

Damn it.

I turn around, ready to bite the head off whoever dares to venture into my inner sanctum, and find my brother Benedict regarding me with an arched brow.

We look so much alike save for the eye color and the goodness that emanates from him just as something wicked brews inside me. I am darkness and shadow. He is golden light. I hear the whispers. I know those that think him a bastard—Benedict himself included. I pay those words little heed. Full brother or half, he is my best and only true friend.

"Welcome home, Bastard," I say. It's a joke between us. We wear our vulnerabilities like armor. It's the way we survive as the lords of the land, all eyes on us.

"That was Wagner, no?" He cocks his head. "You only play that when a woman has you tied in knots."

His memory is keen.

"Dear brother, don't you know? If there is a woman and knots to consider, I am the one doing the tying. Apologies if I offend your holy sensibilities." I eye Benedict's simple clerical garb. My brother is a seminarian, a year away from taking his holy vows and entering the priesthood, much to the eternal pride of our father. When the idea of his virginity is not causing me nightmares, the idea is amusing in the extreme. Benedict is one of the most sought-after men in Europe, and he chooses to marry the church.

I hope God keeps his bed warm.

"What good is the spare to my heir if he is celibate?" Father likes to roar after a drink too many. While he speaks in jest, there is a glimmer of truth.

Benedict takes it all in stride. All he wants to do is please the king—to prove himself worthy of his lineage no matter what the rumors say. When Benedict declared his life belonged to the church, Father was the first to commend him.

How many times have I wondered if a woman could ever tempt him from his path? But he assures me that his destiny is fixed. That the pleasures of the flesh pale in comparison to the rhapsody of the soul.

I have to say, burying my face between Kate's thighs takes me to the gates of heaven. Imagine what burying my cock in her would do.

"I came to bid you good-night and let you know that I'll be taking up residence in the south tower for the foreseeable future."

Benedict long ago laid a claim to the ancient keep on the far northern border of the palace grounds. He prefers its austere environment for prayer and solitude.

"What happened to the Vatican?" I ask him. "Thought you were off to Italy for good."

He laughs softly. "The Vatican City is its own country," he reminds me. "As you should have learned when studying geography."

"Ah, didn't Mrs. Everdeen tutor us on that subject?"

He inclines his head.

"Well, I was too busy studying Mrs. Everdeen in other ways." I smirk. "She had this trick she could do with her tongue that—"

"You are incorrigible, brother," Benedict says. "And yet it is bloody good to see you."

I cross the room and enfold him in a warm bear hug, slapping him on the back. "You too."

"I hear you are to be wed. Is it your bride who has you playing Wagner?"

I shake my head. "The matchmaker." The words are out before I can stop them.

Damn Benedict. His kind eyes make a sinner like me yearn to confess.

He nods thoughtfully. "Sounds like a dilemma."

A flicker of hope lights in me. "You're the scholar in the family."

"Between you and Damien, it wasn't hard to do."

Benedict is also the only one not afraid to acknowledge our younger brother's existence in my presence.

I ignore it this once. "If there's a loophole to the Royal Marriage Decree, a way for me to make my own damned decisions without losing the kingdom, I need you to find it. I am determined not to wed. You know this."

He appears thoughtful. "Such an action will displease our father."

"Yes." And by extension, that will displease my too-good brother. "And Adele," I add. My lips curl into a grin as I know this point will make Benedict my ally.

He brightens at that thought. He and Adele have no love lost. That witch is the only person to ever make my saintly brother lose his temper.

"Very well," he says, a muscle twitching in his jaw at the mention of our stepmother. "I'll look into it."

"You are truly a glorious human. You'll be canonized yet."

He grins at that, but his normally clear green eyes remain dark.

"What's the reason you are back, brother?" My light

tone doesn't mask the hint of probing seriousness. "You haven't said."

His lips tilt in a smile that only I ever get to see, one that isn't all that angelic. "It appears the Lord's wish is to help prevent your sacrament of marriage." He clicks his heels and disappears out the door.

It takes me a moment to realize that he hasn't answered my question at all.

Kate

What the hell was I thinking, placing a wager against someone as strong-willed as Nikolai Lorentz? If there's anything a man like him thrives on, it's the game, and I've just upped the stakes of the one he'd been playing long before I came into the picture—thinking I will get him to play by his own kingdom's rules.

I pace the length of the conference room, the same one where I first met the prince two weeks ago, and the same one where, afterward, the king and queen called me to a private meeting without their son.

Shit.

The door opens, and I freeze midpace only to find Beatrice and another member of the kitchen staff with a silver cart laden with pastries, finger sandwiches and a sterling teapot. Each woman offers me a quick nod as they begin depositing the refreshments on the table.

"Will there be more than the king and queen joining me in here?" I ask nervously, and Beatrice shakes her head.

"No, Miss. These are Queen Adele's favorites. The king orders Her Majesty's most requested finger foods when she's in—" The other woman flashes Beatrice a look, but Beatrice waves her off and crosses over to where I stand. "It's really not my place, Miss, but I think you should know today is the anniversary of Miss Victoria's passing."

I swallow, and my eyes widen. I am to meet with the queen on the anniversary of her daughter's death—the daughter who was betrothed to Nikolai.

The date hadn't registered with me. Of course I knew of Nikolai and Victoria's relationship. The entire continent did. But it had been years since the car crash. It wasn't the type of thing that made news anymore. Nikolai saw to that—*sees* to that every moment he finds himself in the spotlight. Unless the king has any diplomatic dealings that call for broadcast coverage, Nikolai is the family's media darling.

Why, then? Why have my sovereign rulers called me here today, of all days, for a mere check-in on my list of possible brides for the prince?

A throat clears, and Beatrice and I both look up to see the other kitchen servant nodding toward the entrance of the room where Queen Adele stands in the double doorway, flanked by two guards.

She wears an exquisite black dress, long sleeved with a square neckline, the bodice hugging her womanly curves. I can see why King Nikolai was taken with her so soon after Queen Cordelia's death. The woman is a sight to behold, her golden hair in perfect pin curls framing her face, a ruby-studded tiara atop her head. She is elegance and grace, but there is ice in her emerald stare, and I can't help the shiver that makes my hair stand on end.

"That will be all, everyone," she says, and the two

guards, along with Beatrice and her assistant, leave the room, pulling the doors closed behind them.

I bow my head and curtsy as she walks toward the head of the table, and I wait for her to sit. I'm not sure where to seat myself, so like an idiot I ask, "May I pour you some tea, Your Highness?"

"Do sit, Miss Winter," she says, her voice laced with amusement when I expect to hear the remnants of grief. Surely she's come from visiting her daughter's grave. Or perhaps she will be on her way after our meeting.

Our meeting. It's only when I take a seat at the opposite end of the table that I realize the king is nowhere to be seen.

"Will His Highness, King Nikolai, be joining us soon?"

She laughs softly. "The king is away on matters of state business," she says. "It's just the two of us, I'm afraid." She places her palms flat atop the mahogany table. "Don't worry, Miss Winter. I shall be brief."

I nod as the breath catches in my throat. Something about the queen—being in her presence alone—has all my senses on high alert.

"I know how important this job is to you," she drawls, her tone like an animal toying with its prey.

"Yes, Your Highness. It is," I say.

She steeples her fingers before her and grins, the smile not quite reaching her deep green eyes.

"And that you and your sister stand to gain a great deal of fortune if all goes according to plan."

Double my fee *is* a generous offer. "Yes, Your Highness."

She leans forward, and though the length of the table separates us, I flinch at the movement.

"And if you do *not* succeed, your business will be in ruins."

I gasp. To lose the fee promised me would be a devastating blow, but Madeline and I would still be able to come back from it. We'd still—

"Stop trying to rationalize whatever it is you think you're going to say to me, Miss Winter. I'm not in the habit of ruining others—as long as we are on the same side. And I think we both want the same thing, don't we? To see my stepson walk down that aisle and the throne stay in the…immediate family?"

"Yes, of course," I say. I hold her gaze, determined not to flinch again.

Her posture relaxes, but only slightly. "Good. Then all you have to do is keep up business as usual. Seek out all the lovely, appropriate, *deserving* women. Build up Nikolai's image like his father hopes you will."

My teeth grind together in my mouth. Something is off here, but so far she's not asking anything other than what I'm already doing.

"May I ask you a question, Your Highness?"

Her brows rise. She is considering my boldness, no doubt, but then she nods her head.

"Forgive me if I'm being untoward. But are you trying to see to it that I fail or succeed? Because I can't for the life of me figure out why you called this meeting."

This time her eyes light up as her lips curl. "You *will* succeed, Miss Winter."

"How do you know?" I add, deciding to go for broke in my impropriety of speaking my uncensored thoughts in front of my leader.

"Because," she says, standing from her chair. I stand as well. "*I'm* going to find the woman most deserving of a life with my stepson, and we will present her to him when the time is right."

"But my list—"

She shakes her head, closing her eyes as she does. When she looks at me again, I see something so cold in that stare that I shudder. "My match won't be on any such list, but when I've found the one, you'll know. All you have to do is convince Nikolai she's the one, as well." She narrows her eyes at me. "That boy trusts you already. I've seen the way he looks at you. All you have to do is maintain that trust—keep him occupied while I set everything in place. You'll get your doubled fee and maybe even an additional bonus. I get what's rightfully mine and Nikolai gets what he deserves."

"Rightfully yours?" I ask, unable to stop the question even though I know I should not speak out of turn with her.

But the queen doesn't bother to respond.

She plucks a cucumber finger sandwich from the top of a tiered plate and pops it in her mouth, smirking as she devours it. Then she saunters out of the room, not waiting for me to say another word.

Double my fee. A bonus. Or a ruined business if we're not playing for the same side.

Maybe Nikolai does play his games, but he no longer makes the rules.

I wonder now if he ever did.

CHAPTER TEN

Nikolai

I WAKE TO harsh late-morning light striking my sleep-dry eyes. Crimson silk sheets tangle at the base of my four-poster ebony wood bed.

I'm buck naked.

No big surprise there. I never sleep with clothes. This rock-hard morning wood isn't unusual, either. The only strange part to this scenario is that I'm not reaching for my phone. No mad urge within me craves a speed dial to any of my usual female liaisons. There is no shortage of nubile women eager to serve as my royal lover for the morning. But I have made a great effort to ensure that my personal speed dial is discreet and only includes women interested in keeping things horizontal. Commitment types get deleted.

But today is different.

I close my fist around my shaft, circling the tip with my thumb. It's already slick with a bead of pre-cum. Must have been having one hell of a dream. A flash of it glimmers in the back of my mind, Kate's auburn waves spilling over her shoulders, her milk-white breasts rising and falling with her gasps as I bury myself inside her.

I bite on the inside of my cheek. Even the fleeting memory of the tantalizing dream is enough to make me moan out loud.

As if sensing my need, my phone buzzes. But it's no perfectly timed offer from a casual lover. I stare at the name on the screen as all the extra blood in my brain rushes off to pool in my cock.

Kate Winter: Morning, Sunshine. Ready when you are!

I give myself a few more hard pumps, remember how Kate's tangy sweet pussy tastes, and my hips buck off the mattress. "Oh, I'm ready, Pet."

The phone buzzes again. I'm with X.

X. The mention of my personal guard almost throws me off my game. He is like another brother. We even shared women in depraved threesomes, once upon a time when I was younger and even wilder than I am now. But that doesn't mean I want to share Kate. A muffled growl rises in my throat. I don't want to share her with anyone else in the world.

Strange. Normally I'm a love-the-one-you're-with kind of guy. After I'm with a woman, it's out of sight and out of mind. But with Kate it's different. There is an unfamiliar pull inside me to know more than her body, but I have no idea what to do with this—feeling.

The notion leaves me unsettled. I remove my hand from my dick and text her back.

Nikolai: Still in bed.

Kate: What!?!?!?!? Are you coming?

Nikolai: Not without you…

Kate: Excuse me?

Nikolai: A real man never comes first, Pet.

Kate: OMG

Nikolai: ;)

Kate: You did not just winky face me.

Nikolai: What are you going to do about it? ;)

Kate: I've just eaten my weight in Beatrice's white chocolate scones waiting for you or I'd march up there and drag you down myself.

Nikolai: I have a king-size bed. Perfect place to sleep off a food coma.

Kate: I have an heiress to a screw company waiting at the airfield.

Nikolai: ?

Kate: Your next date is Regina Bjorn. Her father is Vlad Bjorn, owner of Big Bjorn Screws, one of Edenvale's largest exports. We are meeting her at the royal hangar at noon. You're flying her in your personal helicopter.

Nikolai: I'm so screwed.

Kate: ;)

I swing my bare feet to the cold floorboards, my grin from our banter quickly morphing into a sneer. I know Vlad Bjorn. He is titled with a minor barony and is a large man with blotchy skin. He calls himself the Big Screw, but in my opinion he resembles a stick of bologna. I know he has twelve daughters but can't picture any of their faces at the moment. That fact alone leaves me numb. I don't want to fly this Regina anywhere, not when I could be flirting with my feisty matchmaker, who can't learn that my brother Benedict is looking for a loophole to break the Royal Marriage Decree. Until then I must play my hand well by making nice with the dates Kate sets up for me. Not to raise so much as an eyebrow of suspicion.

Lucky for me, I am a most excellent actor.

Kate

My eyes widen as I stare out the window toward the airfield. I knew the palace grounds were substantial, but each time I see something new, it still catches me off guard. My world is so small compared to his.

"Impressed?" Nikolai whispers in my ear, his warm breath sending tingles all the way to my toes.

I nod. "This *car* would barely fit in my apartment. The concept of an airfield is a lot to take in."

"You never listed your terms," he says softly, his voice like velvet, and I know exactly what he means.

I turn to face him, and he barely backs away. My heart races as my eyes meet his.

"Well," I say, keeping my voice steady. "I know money—or anything of material value—is of no consequence to you, which I guess bodes well for me since I have nothing of material value to offer."

"Kate—" he starts, but I shake my head. I don't want him to apologize for his wealth, nor will I apologize for my lack thereof.

"Nikolai. We come from different worlds, and that's okay." His eyes darken at this, and I wish I had the time to ask him what he's thinking, but the car slows, and I know we're approaching the hangar. "And because I'm going to win," I tease, trying to lighten whatever heaviness has taken over his features, "I'll keep it simple."

"Simple?" he asks, raising a brow, painting on that prince of a smile, one I know he is readying for the heiress.

"A favor," I say simply. "If I win—which I plan to do—you do me one favor. If *you* win—which is highly unlikely—then you get to ask a favor of me."

"Are there limits?" he asks. "To what we can ask?"

I shake my head. "No limits on my end. If you are not wed by your birthday, you can ask me for anything you want. Do *you* have any limits?"

"None," he says quickly, his voice suddenly rough. "Ask me anything right now, Kate. Tell me what you'd want from me."

But the car halts, effectively ending our conversation.

"Time for you to fly to Zurich," I say, forcing a smile.

"It's just lunch," he says. "You and X should—"

"I am *not* tagging along on any more dates. If you want to bring X, fine. I'm only here to make sure you aren't late and to remind you to be a gentleman."

He winks at me. "Darling, have you forgotten who I am? I'll do nothing of the sort."

"Nikolai..."

He kisses me on the cheek, effectively shutting me up.

"No worries, Pet. I'll be on my best behavior."

I groan. "That's what I'm afraid of."

Nikolai's door opens, and X stands ready to usher him out of the vehicle and to the hangar.

"I'll be back by dusk," he says on his way out. "And I'd like you here when I arrive."

He doesn't wait for me to protest but assumes I'll obey his every whim.

What if I had plans tonight? I want to ask—even though I don't. As much as it warms me from within that he wants to see me this evening, I can't help but feel like the afterthought that I am and can only ever be.

X joins me in the car, and I watch as Nikolai strides toward Regina Bjorn, a regal, platinum-haired beauty who stands in front of a BMW with windows tinted so black I'm not even sure you can see through them at all.

Zurich was my idea, to have him take her to her mother's homeland, a place I learned she hadn't visited since childhood but had always missed. He'd score points in the thoughtfulness department before they'd even left the helipad, which I glance at in front of the hangar. Nikolai holds her hand as she climbs into the helicopter. Her azure scarf billows in the breeze, floating against Nikolai's crisp white oxford—a picture-perfect couple.

My breath hitches.

I knock on the window in front of me, and X lowers the glass.

"Shall I take you home, Miss?"

The confines of the apartment that doubles as the home office for Happy Endings do not comfort me, especially if it means the third degree from Maddie. If I don't want to think about Nikolai on his date, I certainly don't want to *talk* about Nikolai on his date. So I decide to do something I rarely do—something for *me*.

"X," I say, my mood brightening. "We're going to the cinema."

"Miss, there is a private theater in the palace—"

"Absolutely not. No palace. No royal treatment. Just you and me and that car-chase-with-tons-of-explosions action film that premiered last weekend."

"But, Miss—the palace theater has that film or any other—"

I lean through the open partition. "No. Royal. Treatment."

He clears his throat and starts the engine. "As you wish, Miss Kate."

He backs away from the hangar as the propeller blades begin to spin. And when the helicopter lifts off the ground, I allow myself a few seconds to marvel that the strong hands controlling that beast of a machine have touched me in ways no other man has.

Then I sink into my seat.

"Thank you, X." I hand him my phone. "And maybe my Fall Out Boy playlist while we drive. Crank up the volume so I can't hear myself think." Drowning out my thoughts seems preferable to drowning *in* them. I reach for a bottle and glass from the minibar across from my seat. "And—and I'm going to have some of the prince's cognac even though it's before noon."

"As you wish, Miss."

Seconds later the music blares.

X's eyes remain on the road as we approach the palace gates, but I swear I see a devilish grin take over his stoic countenance. Yet as quickly as it appears, it is gone.

I pour myself a drink and then take a long sip. After a few seconds I tip my head back and laugh.

"No royal treatment," I say with a snort. "I'm in a Rolls-Royce with a private driver and a bottle of cognac. And I have to return at dusk to meet up with the prince." I snort again, but damn it, the laughter feels good.

No royal treatment indeed.

CHAPTER ELEVEN

Nikolai

THE MOUNTAINS EN ROUTE to Zurich are as sculpted as Regina Bjorn's high cheekbones, and yet the experience feels empty. Emotionally at least. Regina has done a damn good job of filling the airspace, making it clear that she knows a thing or two about screwing.

"It is, after all, the family business," she chatters into the microphone with a giggle. We both wear helmets with headsets.

"Nothing about that innuendo is remotely appealing," I mutter and grip the cyclical stick that gives me control of the aircraft.

My surly comment flies straight over her head. As does anything else I say for the rest of our time together—unless it's an attempt to feign interest in her father's company.

Screws.

By the time we return to the Royal Airfield, landing with the setting sun, I'm convinced that I've endured paper cuts more enjoyable than Regina Bjorn.

Kate paired me with this woman through her matchmaking service? What does this say about me and the persona that I have cultivated with such care? Has the shallow, arrogant, vain Prince Nikolai finally become Mr. Hyde, overriding the respectable Dr. Jekyll? Is the facade I've so long shown the world really the man I want to be? I've nearly convinced myself the mask is real. But when Kate looks at me, it's as if she can see someone else. The person that I might have been if life hadn't kicked me in the teeth with a stiletto then had my youngest brother drive it off a cliff.

The thought unsettles me, and I push it from my mind as we exit the helicopter. I escort Regina back to her driver. She still talks of—what else?—screws. In the last hours I've endured lectures about cap screws, machine screws, tag screws, setscrews and—I shit you not—self-tapping screws.

A few weeks ago I would have been able to turn the day's conversation into an activity that required no words at all—unless it was Regina purring my bloody name. Now I hope those self-tapping wonders are Regina's favorite because I don't know anyone who could stay awake through one of her conversations long enough to get it up.

When I wish her good-night, I am not entirely convinced she notices.

The Rolls is parked in my usual spot. As I stride closer, eager to put distance between myself and the Heiress of Screws, I am surprised to hear music playing. It's an American classic, "Sweet Caroline." More to the point, the two people in the car are belting out the words—and X can apparently more than hold a tune. This man… I shake my head. He's full of surprises. Not only is he an expert tattoo artist responsible for all the tribal ink on my body, he's also a ninth-degree Grand

Master black belt in Tae Kwon Do, and my on-again, off-again threesome wingman. Now he can harmonize better than Neil Diamond?

Sneaky fuck.

Who the hell *is* X? So often I've asked myself this, but it is to no avail. X has been my bodyguard since I reached maturity. I barely remember life without him. And yet I know nothing of him when he's not in my immediate presence, while he knows all there is of me.

I guess he can add charismatic crooner to his résumé.

I open the door, and he and Kate both clam up, staring at me.

"I didn't know you were back yet," she says, clutching what appears to be a giant bucket of popcorn.

"You didn't hear the chopper blades?" I inquire, lifting an eyebrow. I fly a Eurocopter Mercedes-Benz, the most pimped-out helicopter in the world, able to get high and fly fast. For one not to notice such an aircraft, well—what the hell could pry her interest from awaiting my arrival?

I scowl to myself. Perhaps I *am* the pompous persona I've cultivated.

"Sorry. It's the Golden Oldies Hour on Royal Radio. Our favorite," she said.

"Our?" My eyebrow goes higher.

"Sir." X is matter-of-fact and unapologetic as he starts the engine. "Would you like to take a seat?"

"I'd like to know who you are and what you've done with my bodyguard," I shoot back as an unexpected wave of possessive jealousy rolls between my clenched shoulder blades.

"Was your outing with Miss Bjorn satisfactory?"

Kate asks, popping a piece of popcorn into her mouth with wide eyes.

"No. And where the hell did you get that?"

She pops another kernel into her mouth. "We went to the movies. They were showing the live action *Beauty and the Beast* at the discount theater and X had never seen it."

"An oversight he must be happy to have rectified," I snap.

Kate shrugs. "I was prepared to share with him my love of all things fast and furious, but the Disney classic won out. Apparently X is impressed by royalty. Me, not so much." She bites back a grin, and all I can do is bite back my own rage.

X's eyes shoot to mine in the rearview, and I glare out the window. Stupid to be jealous of my bodyguard. But the entire day I suffered with Regina *Bore*, he was with Kate. Enjoying himself. Enjoying *her*. I've shared women with X in the past, but this is one time that I don't want to. I don't want to share her with *anyone*. The idea of her with another man, even if I'm there as well, makes my stomach turn over as my fingers curl into themselves.

I stare back at her as white-hot possession shoots through me.

Mine.

The word is powerful and pure. My blood pounds with the echo. *Mine. Mine. Mine.*

This is the truth. And it's time she knows it.

"X, to the palace."

"I need to get back to the office," Kate protests. "If your second date was another bust, then I need to review lucky number three and figure out a game plan."

"I want to use the back entrance," I continue as if she hasn't spoken. A vague headache pounds in my temples. I want to drop the pretense for two seconds. I will never marry. I'm not made for the institution, and Kate is wasting her time.

That shouldn't be my problem, but I don't want her to leave. At least not yet. I want to enjoy the pleasure of her company a little while longer.

"Sir?" X asks, and I know what he really means. "Are you sure about this?"

No woman has ever accompanied me back to the palace, to my private quarters. Not until now.

I nod my head. "And make it fast."

Kate

"Where are the king and queen this fine evening?" Nikolai asks X as we pull to a side of the palace I haven't seen before.

"In Paris until tomorrow for the queen's—" he coughs "—rejuvenation treatments."

Nikolai grins at me. "Do you need to let your sister know you won't be coming home this evening?"

I cross my arms and narrow my eyes. "I don't have a curfew, *Your Highness*. But I do have work to do if we are going to make the perfect match, so I really should—"

"Stay," he says, the grin fading, those gray eyes dark with something too intense to deny. Because I feel it too—have felt it since he left for Zurich despite the comfort of X's presence and our day of distraction.

I won't ask him why. Or what this means. I won't let logic override the ache in my belly. I can do this and not endanger the business. I force myself to believe it because the word is already forming on my lips.

"Okay," I answer.

Nikolai's door opens, and X stands at the ready. The man is the epitome of stealth. I didn't even realize he'd exited the vehicle.

Nikolai turns toward the opened door. "Miss Winter will be staying this evening, X."

X nods. "A moment alone with your guest, please, Your Highness. I shall then escort her to your quarters."

Nikolai laughs quietly. "A bit bold today, aren't we, X?"

X nods but doesn't crack a smile. "When it's called for, Your Highness."

Nikolai faces me again, gently grabbing my palm and bringing it to his lips. "See you soon," he whispers, and then he's gone.

Moments later my door opens, and X offers a hand to help me out of the vehicle.

"Let me guess," I say, as he leads me through a small door and into a dimly lit stairwell. "You want to finish our Neil Diamond duet."

No smile or any indication that only several minutes ago the two of us could have turned every chair on *The Voice*. Instead he simply holds out an arm for me to grab as we begin to ascend the steep stairs.

"The prince," he says, "is very private."

I snort.

"What the world sees in the media is what he wants them to see, Miss. And while I am not at liberty to divulge his past, I can say as much as this. Save for Victoria, the queen's late daughter, no woman has ascended these stairs. Not before—and not since."

There is no time for me to respond as we reach a small landing at the top, a tall oak door—partially ajar—before us. He nods for me to enter, and I do. I hear the door click shut behind me and turn to see X standing with his back to it, the faintest hint of a smile on his face. Then, as quick as a blink, he steps to his left, where soft curtains billow beside an open window—and he leaps through it like we aren't on the third story of a palace.

I yelp.

Nikolai rounds the corner, a bottle of Moët in one hand, two crystal flutes in the other.

"Let me guess," he says. "X took the window."

My hand covers my mouth as I nod, imagining my silver-fox companion splattered against the brick pavers below.

Nikolai laughs and shakes his head. "He often prefers scaling the brick to the stairs. Sometimes I wonder who X was before he came here, but I've learned to not question the man's abilities and thank the stars we're on the same team." He moves closer, his feet bare beneath the dark denim of his jeans and his now-wrinkled oxford unbuttoned. "He's fine. I promise."

"I'm not looking out that window," I say, goose bumps raising the hairs on my bare arms. The sundress was perfect for the day, but now that the sun has set, I shiver in the open-air breeze. "I'll take your word for it."

Nikolai nods toward the direction from which he came.

"You're cold," he says. "Come. Let me warm you up."

I follow him around a corner and note a small galley kitchen with dark marble counters, a sturdy wooden

table—round—with four high-backed chairs beyond
the breakfast bar. I don't have time to take in the modest living space other than a baby grand piano against
a floor-to-ceiling window beyond a leather couch. The
next thing I know, I'm walking through another door
and into my prince's bedroom.

He sets the bottle and flutes on a night table and
turns back to me. His strong hands run the length of
my arms, warming me from the outside in. I let out
a breath.

"Why am I here, Nikolai?" I can't hold out any longer, my curiosity getting the best of me. My chest tightens at the thought of his answer.

He kisses my neck, and my head falls back. A small
sigh escapes my lips.

"I don't want to share you," he says against my skin,
his lips making their way up to my jaw, then my cheek.

"But I haven't been—" I stop myself before telling
him that I have not been with any other man since he
first laid his hands on me—that for two years before
that there hadn't been anyone, either.

His mouth finds mine, and my lips part, inviting
him in—craving the taste of him like I didn't know
I could.

"I don't like that X got to see a side of you today
that I've never seen."

The sentence comes out almost as a growl, and my
breath hitches.

"It was a movie," I whisper. "Not a helicopter ride
to another country for an intimate lunch." I don't regret the words—or laying my jealousy out before him,
not when he is blatantly doing the same. I want him,

more than I've been able to admit, and right now I'm ready to give him all of me in return.

He backs toward the four-poster ebony bed, red silk sheets pulled back to reveal the space where his body last lay. I grin against his lips.

"What?" he asks, feeling the change in my expression.

"No one comes in to clean? To make your bed, Your Highness?"

He sits on the edge of the mattress, pulling me close so I straddle his lap.

"No one enters other than those closest to me," he says, his eyes dark with need. "And I want you closest, Kate. Tonight I want you more than anyone else."

I answer him by unbuttoning his shirt the rest of the way and sliding it down his arms. He closes his eyes and breathes in deep as my fingers trace the lines of ink on his shoulder, as they circle the tattoo of a compass that rests above his heart.

"It's beautiful," I say, a slight tremor in my voice. "*You're* beautiful, Nikolai."

He opens his eyes and wordlessly lifts my dress over my head so I'm left in nothing but my white lace panties.

"You're exquisite," he says. Then he takes one of my breasts into his mouth. I arch against him. "Finer than any woman who bears a title." His tongue swirls around the peaked nipple of my other breast, and I gasp. "Open your eyes and look at me," he says, and I obey. "No matter what I do, you *see* me."

I cradle his beautiful face in my palms. "I do."

"And you *want* me," he says.

I nod.

"*Only* me."

I nod again, taking each of his palms in mine and pressing them to my breasts. "Only you."

"I'll win our wager," he says with a grin. "I will not walk down the aisle."

"You *will* marry," I remind him and swallow back the reality of what that means.

"Not tonight, though." He falls onto the bed, pulling me over him.

"No," I say. "Not tonight."

CHAPTER TWELVE

Nikolai

FOR HOW LONG has my soul been trapped in a vise of loneliness? For years I have passed through countless nights as restless and insatiable as a vampire. Instead of feeding on mortal blood, I devoured what distraction and comfort was available in the form of sexual release—the more depraved, the better.

I take and take and take with a relentlessness matched only by my many lovers who are eager to use me in turn for the proximity to limitless power and wealth.

But tonight? All I want is to give. Kate Winter shall experience nothing less than absolute, exquisite pleasure.

She is stretched above me. My hands roam the soft swells of her body, the dip of her small hourglass waist. Her loose curls tumble over my face, forming a curtain of fire. Again I am stricken by the paradox—Miss Winter, whose hair burns brighter than the sun, whose undeniable beauty burns my heart.

"Are you sure this is a good idea?" she whispers, and as her lips part, I catch a glimpse of her teeth, her tongue. Oh yes, that pink clever tongue, which swirled around my cock until I nearly forgot my birthright. And that was in a hurried riverside tryst. Tonight the hours spread before us, and I intend to put each one to good use.

"A good idea?" I give my head a single shake. "No, Pet. It is *the best* idea."

A hitched breath escapes her perfect lips as I cradle her face in my hands. My mouth finds hers, and our groans collide. I place my palms over her breasts again, and her heart careens against my hand. My thumbs circle her nipples before teasing them with a flick. She gasps in appreciation, sinking her nails deep into my biceps. I coax her forward.

Her breasts tumble into my face. I suck one gorgeous nipple into my mouth, then the other, feasting as if she is languorously feeding me champagne grapes. One small press of my teeth against her sensitive flesh, a teasing nip, and she arches, her pelvis rocking over mine.

I snarl from need mixed with acute frustration. Tonight I had planned to take it slow, savor every last inch of her body, worship her skin with my tongue. But animal that I am, lust consumes me, and a deeper feeling, an urgency comes over me to be *home*, as if her body is the safe harbor in the violent black storms that have rocked my world for so long. Turbulence has since become my new normal.

"My turn," she whispers, moving over me, traveling the ridges of my flexed abdomen with her pouty lips. Then lower, until she reaches my belt buckle, unhooks it, and with a pop of a button and the grind of a zipper, my entire proud length is revealed.

She takes me by the root and swirls her tongue around the end. "Mmm," she murmurs. "So good."

I prop myself up on my elbows, letting her take me for a few wet strokes. "Fuck," I groan.

"You like that?" she asks in a flirtatious tone, before adding, "Your *Majesty*."

Naughty minx.

"Hell yes, I do, Pet. And you know what I'll like even more?"

She arches a brow in question.

"Tasting you at the same time." I reach down and with one deft motion flip her around so her pert ass is in my face. "Spread those thighs for me," I growl, slapping one cheek, and she moans loudly, parting her legs wide enough to let me see the sheen on her intimate flesh.

"You are so goddamn gorgeous," I groan and slam her against me. With both hands I give her hips a firm rock, encouraging her to fuck my face, seizing her pleasure as she works over my cock, taking every inch that I have to give.

I flex my tongue over her swollen folds, making sure her clit is well-attended, and when her breath grows ragged, I press harder, giving her hearty licks, writing my name on the soaked, silky skin, marking my territory with flourishing circles and swirls, an intimate calligraphy.

As she falls apart, I plunge my tongue deep inside her tight hole, ravage her with smooth strokes, hinting at the delirious euphoria that is about to be hers.

"Nikolai, oh, God, Nikolai," she gasps, rising up to sit on the back of her heels, spastically jerking then grinding over me in a slow, rhythmic, figure-eight fashion. "Oh God! Your Highness!" She gasps. "Fuck me harder!"

I could come this very second. Sweet, sweet Kate has one filthy mouth. And I obediently comply. The bed shakes. Someday I'll control this entire land, but right now this firecracker is begging to be ruled. Before I take what is mine, I plunge my full face against her pretty pink pussy.

Tonight is about the journey, not the destination. I lick and fuck her until she is dripping and on all fours, hot, tangy juices running down my chin. Two orgasms. Three. Fuck. I lose count of how many I give her. But now my cock is so thick, the need so intense, that I need to join her in this mad passion. Ours won't be a mindless rutting. A fleeting pleasure.

I freeze as the realization takes hold.

There is a chance that entering her will tear asunder the very fiber of my soul.

Kate

I don't know what's come over me. I've never spoken like that. Not to Jean-Luc. Not to anyone. But this man—this man turns me into my basest self. A woman in need who will do or say whatever it takes to satisfy the hunger. And I hunger for Nikolai Lorentz, with everything that I am.

He lifts his head from between my legs, his dark hair a beautiful mess of ravaged waves.

"I need you," he says, his voice strained. "Fuck, Kate. I *need* you."

There is something akin to pain in his words, an

ache I'm not expecting, and the animal in me gives way to something else entirely so that all I can do is nod.

He stands from the bed, and despite how hard I already came, I need him inside me. I need *him*, too.

How can any good come of feeling like this?

He disappears into the bathroom, and I hear the faucet run. When I can't stand not knowing how long it will be until he returns, I follow him in there, not caring that he knows how desperate I am to keep him close.

His head dips toward the sink as he splashes water over his face again and again. I rest my palm on his back, and he shudders.

"Nikolai," I say softly.

He straightens enough for me to see his beautiful face in the mirror.

"I thought I could clear my thoughts. I thought I could cleanse away this feeling." He shakes his head. "But I *need* you," he says again to our mirrored selves. "I'm not supposed to *need* anyone."

I see the foil packet on the counter, grab it and tear it open.

"Look at me," I say. "No hiding behind a reflection."

The muscles in his shoulders and back flex as he moves, and when our eyes meet, I don't hesitate as I roll the condom down his thick, pulsing length. He sucks in a breath.

"Remember," I say. "No matter what sort of mask you give to the rest of the world, I *see* you."

As much as this man turns me to animal, I shift to caring lover just as quickly. Because who truly takes care of a prince?

He dips his head toward mine but stops before our lips barely touch.

"You're the only one who can."

And then he kisses me with such tenderness I have to fight back tears. I rise to the tips of my toes, and he nudges my entrance. I grab the base of his shaft and urge him inside. His palms clamp against my thighs, and he lifts me. I wrap my legs around his waist as he sinks into my warmth, and a growl tears from his lips.

Nikolai walks with me like this until we're back at the bed. He lays me on the elegant silk sheet and climbs over me, burying himself as deep as he can go.

I cry out. Not from pleasure or pain but from the undeniable ache of both. The walls around my heart crumble to dust, letting my prince inside.

My prince.

"My prince." This time I say it aloud as he slides out and back in again—slow, controlled, deliberate. He claims me with each thrust. Heart and soul.

My prince.

My prince.

My prince.

His lips are strong and fierce against mine. Each sweep of his tongue is a taste sweeter than any confection and richer than the royal coffers.

The pressure builds, and his momentum picks up. My muscles throb around him as I feel him pulse inside me. So close. He's so close. But I know he's waiting for me.

And because he knows me like no man ever has, he knows what is necessary to send me over the edge.

He slips a hand between us, at the place where two

bodies become one, and presses his thumb to my swollen clit. I cry out again and again and again.

He roars as he tumbles off the cliff with me, shuddering above me until we both shatter into a million pieces.

He opens his eyes and traps me in his steel gaze.

"My *queen*," he says before collapsing beside me.

I stroke his sweat-dampened hair as he peppers my shoulder with kisses so achingly tender. I try not to take his words to heart. What we have is only temporary, until I find him a proper bride.

He combs my hair out of my face, his fingers grazing my chin. "My beautiful, fiery winter queen," he says, and I start to wish those words to be truth, though I know full well they never could be. Even if he would marry, a commoner like me could never be in the running.

"Your *what*?" I hear, and gasp when I see a figure looming over us where we lie.

Nikolai turns his head lazily toward our intruder.

"Fucking hell, Christian," he says with nothing more than mild annoyance in his words. "How in God's name did you get in here? And do you ever bloody knock?"

The man steps closer, a muscle ticking in his chiseled jaw. "Give me one good reason why I shouldn't lay you out like the bloody prick you are. Royal law or not, you know I can fucking do it, and it looks like your shadow isn't here to stop me."

I suck in a breath. Am I about to witness a royal brawl? Or worse—get caught in the middle of it? Regardless of my ability to do so or not, a fierce urge to protect my prince takes hold.

"Who are you?" I ask, but the man ignores me, his gaze still fixed on His Royal Highness.

Nikolai sits up, not at all concerned that he's conducting this conversation completely naked. In fact, he uses his other hand to free his princely cock from its condom.

"Come now, Christian. Answer the lady's question as you know I'm too bored to keep answering yours."

The man clenches his teeth. "Lady?" he says. "I'll do no such thing. But you can bloody tell me why you called this commoner *queen*."

Nikolai glances back at me and winks, and with that tiny gesture the intimacy of our connection falls away.

He laughs. "If you'd been given the royal treatment like I had, you'd bow to the woman who performed such a deed and call her your sovereign, as well."

I know this act. Something about this man—this Christian—instills a quiet fear in the prince, one that causes him to protect our connection. To protect *me*.

"I'm hungry, Your Highness. Can I fix you a snack?"

I slide off the edge of the bed, taking the sheet with me as a robe as I brush past our visitor.

"That would be lovely, Pet."

I grin at the term of endearment as I make my way to the kitchen. Only when I'm out of the room do the pieces start to click in place.

I know that man. Christian. Christian *Wurtzer*.

He is the Baron of Rosegate, the disputed land between Edenvale and our ancient enemies to the north, the Kingdom of Nightgardin. For now Rosegate is under King Nikolai's protection and rule. I squeeze my eyes shut, remembering that the baron also has a supermodel sister. Her face has been splashed across the tabloids almost as much as Nikolai's. Sometimes *together*. Whatever his visit entails, it cannot be good.

And despite what just occurred in Nikolai's room before our interruption, it's only now that I feel royally screwed.

CHAPTER THIRTEEN

Nikolai

"JESUS." CHRISTIAN PACES my room, disgust marring his features. I find a pair of trousers and yank them on. "I'm a fucking idiot. How much time have I wasted worrying that I'd been an overhasty judge, that maybe my little sister, as shallow and conniving as she is, and as depraved and arrogant as you are, had made an unexpected love match?"

He tears a hand through his clipped blond hair. "Instead you're up to your usual tricks, except now you're bedding women in the prince's wing. So much for all your high-minded talk about keeping your chamber as a sanctuary. Now any gold-digging sex kitten can—"

He ceases speaking. Mostly because my hand closes on his throat and squeezes. X once told me he could break a man's neck with a simple flick of the wrist. Good thing he refused to share the trick because, so help me, I would use it against my old friend for besmirching what happened between Kate and me in this room tonight. Our lovemaking was by turns savage and sensual, raw and romantic, two sides of a single emotion, one that hums through me like liquid gold.

I don't dare give it an official name. I don't even think too hard on the word's existence because it feels so fragile, like a soap bubble that could pop in a brisk wind.

Christian's feet kick at the empty air because even as my feelings toward Kate beckon from a place of light, darkness still owns my soul. And my friend dares to condescend an amazing woman such as she.

"Please," he wheezes, hands clawing uselessly at my strength. "Nikolai." He may be skilled in a boxing ring, but I have undiluted fury on my side.

"I don't need a goddamn bodyguard to deal with you, *Baron*. I could break your neck as easily as I could break the alliance with Rosegate," I grind out. "How many hours would it take for Nightgardin to invade if I call off our military protection?"

There is the sound of wood sliding along a groove. Then a warning hand on my shoulder. "Put him down," X's quietly authoritative voice insists.

"Thought I told you to quit using secret passages," I say, releasing Christian and letting him tumble to the floor, gasping for oxygen.

X shakes with noiseless laughter. He doesn't so much as smile, but I know he is amused.

"Don't you get claustrophobic in there?" I ask. The palace is riddled with secret chambers, a veritable rabbit warren within the walls. X seems to liken them to his own personal sanctum.

"After the month I spent as a prisoner in the Russian nuclear sub in the Arctic Sea, the passages here are as roomy as a Versailles ballroom, Your Highness."

"Jesus. Who are you?" I ask him, and not for the first time. I'm never entirely sure if the guy is joking.

"What are you going to do with him?" Per usual, X

evades my question to gesture at Christian, who now pushes himself to standing.

"He disrespected Kate," I snap.

Christian stares at me, eyes wide. "Your face, when you say her name. You *feel* something for this woman. Don't you? I never thought it possible."

"I don't owe you—or anyone, for that matter—any explanations," I remind him. I might sound arrogant as hell, but I never denied that I am a royal prick.

"Your Highness," he says, bowing his head. "I apologize for barging in on you. And for assuming the worst. I actually came to warn you about Catriona, in the vain hope that you and she had forged a connection. After you didn't call, it appears she has gone sour. She had delusions of herself on the Edenvale throne. And I thought that if there was any chance you *did* feel something for her… But I know the truth, that Catriona is only capable of loving herself. Still, she is my sister. When I saw you with—"

"Kate," I say, before he calls her a commoner again and I *do* rip his throat out.

"Of course," he says. "Kate. I just wasn't expecting you felt something for another."

"Thank you," I say curtly. I am not yet ready to forgive, but I appreciate the warning.

I don't have time for Catriona's petty scheming. What I said to Kate tonight was the truth.

She is my addiction; I can't stay away. Every kiss, every caress, every damn moment in her presence hits my body like a drug. I can't seem to get enough and crave fix after fix. It's not that I want her so much as I *need* her. There must be a way to make her my queen and keep my royal inheritance.

Kate

I open the stainless-steel refrigerator in Nikolai's kitchen to find nothing but a bowl of strawberries that look freshly cut.

"They go perfectly with the champagne."

I yelp and almost lose my sheet—the only thing covering my naked body—to find X using a pocket square to clean what looks like berry juice—or possibly blood—from a small knife. I opt to believe it is the former. When he's done, he slips the knife into a sheath inside his suit jacket.

"How did you…? I mean, where did you…?" I glance toward an open window near the grand piano across the great room, but X shakes his head.

"Not tonight, Miss. My travels are *within* the walls this evening rather than without."

I shake my own head and decide not to press the issue. Instead I tuck my sheet tight around me and remove the bowl of berries from the fridge, cradling them against my body. I inhale and sigh.

"How do these smell so good?" I ask, my mouth watering. "I can already taste them."

X reaches into another coat pocket and hands me my cell phone.

"The reason I left the prince alone with the baron. You seem to have missed a call. Also, my apologies for him interrupting you and His Highness. Save for his brother Benedict, Christian Wurtzer is the only one with unrestricted security clearance to the annex, an oversight that will soon be remedied." The corner of his mouth twitches into the ghost of a smile. "The strawberries are a gift. I thought you and the prince might need a bit of—sustenance."

X dips his head in a mild bow and disappears around a corner. I hear the sound of what must be a sliding door on a track and then what I swear is a chuckle coming from within the very walls.

Who is that guy?

The caller identification on my phone steals my attention from the mystery of X. My sister. It's not even eight o'clock. I know I told Nikolai I don't have a curfew, but maybe Maddie is worried after all. I ignore her voice mail and move straight to calling her back.

"Oh, Katie, thank God," she says when she answers.

"I'm okay," I tell her. "I guess I should have called. I'm with Nikolai and—"

"It's Grandmother," she says, and all the air rushes out of my lungs with her utterance of those two words.

"Is she—?"

"She's still with us," Maddie says quickly. "But do you remember the cough she had last time I visited? It turns out it was the onset of pneumonia. They started her on medication, but she wasn't responding. We're at the Royal Hospital. She's on a respirator and IV meds. They say she can recover, but, Katie—the money it will cost for all of this. We're barely making our rent at the moment. Can they not pay you a small advance?"

I swallow back the lump in my throat. "Can we get by for two more months?" I ask.

"If we're very careful," she says. "Maybe." Her voice sounds ready to crack. Poor Maddie. She's shouldered so much responsibility since our parents died. Too much.

I take a deep breath and back myself into a corner of the kitchen, a feeble attempt at privacy.

"As long as I get Nikolai down the aisle, we get double our fee."

I hear her gasp. "But what if you don't?" she asks.

I shake my head. "That won't matter. He will marry. I'm sure of it."

Nikolai won't let the kingdom slip away from his family. As much as he embraces the part of the careless playboy, I know deep down he is a man of duty, which means he *will* have to choose a bride—one who is fit to rule beside him. There is no one better than me to find his perfect match, even if it's only perfect on paper.

As much as the thought kills me, I can't let down my own family. My grandmother was there for me and my sister in our darkest hour. She deserves nothing less from us in kind. To see out her final days in peace and comfort.

"I trust you," Maddie says.

"I won't let you down." I step out of the kitchen and glance toward Nikolai's room and see our uninvited guest on his way toward me. "I have to go," I say.

"Okay. I'll be with Gran all day tomorrow. Only one visitor is allowed at a time. Relieve me in the evening?"

"Of course," I tell her. "I'll be there by five. But I won't be home tonight," I add. "Love you, Maddie." And then I end the call before she can question where I am—before the guilt for not being with Gran now can set in. Because I know what happened between Nikolai and me wasn't just sex.

He called me his queen.

Christian offers me a slight nod as he walks by but

says nothing before letting himself out the apartment's front door.

I pad into Nikolai's room, strawberries in hand. He sits on the edge of his bed, hair rumpled and jeans on but unbuttoned. He pops the bottle of champagne and fills the two flutes.

"Sorry about that, Pet." He offers me a glass.

I set the strawberries on the night table and take it willingly. He pulls me onto his lap and then lifts his own glass, tapping the crystal against mine.

"Stay the night," he says.

I nod, and when I lift my glass to drink, the sheet loosens and falls below my breasts.

"My God, you are beautiful," he says, and I don't bother covering myself again.

He sets down his flute and plucks a strawberry from the bowl, bringing it to my lips. I bite, and juice dribbles onto my lips and my chin. Nikolai kisses me, licking my skin clean. I swallow the rest of my champagne in one sip, the bubbles tickling my tongue, and I'm swept away in a giddiness I've never felt before.

He lays me out on the bed, unwrapping me from the sheet as if I am a gift.

"I'm yours," I say. And we make love again, this time achingly yet wonderfully slow, and I know when he buries himself in me again and again that I'm in trouble. *Big* trouble.

I must help him marry another.

Both of our futures depend on it.

In the morning I slide out from the crook of his arm. I kiss the inked compass above his heart and silently wish for it to point us both in the right direction.

X is surprisingly absent this morning, so I exit the prince's quarters as discreetly as possible, leaving him a note that I've gone for a walk.

I need to clear my head.

Soon after I leave the secluded wing, I find a chapel on the outskirts of the grounds. Perhaps someone inside can offer guidance when I have no direction of my own.

I enter to find the place empty but for the rows of pews. A few moments of silence will do me good, as well.

When I take a seat in the rear, I bow my head and close my eyes.

So... I've never actually done this, I think, rationalizing that if there is some higher power, he or she can hear my thoughts. No need to speak them aloud. *But I have loved. It was a good love, but not a great one. I know that now. Because my chest—my body—doesn't feel like it can contain what I have for Nikolai. But whatever this is will fade. It must. We've only known each other for a few short weeks. And he must marry another.*

"I'm frightened of what I feel," I say aloud.

"That which scares us is the most important to face."

The deep voice comes from behind, and I suck in a breath.

"God?" I ask, afraid to face whoever is chuckling. But I'm being a fool, so I turn.

"Not exactly the risen Lord, but I like to think we're close." A dark-haired man, dressed head to toe in black, stares at me with the loveliest green eyes. He wears the white collar of the seminary.

"Oh! Father!" I stand quickly, bumping my knee

on the pew in front of me, and hiss out a curse before covering my mouth. "I'm so sorry," I say.

The man smiles, and his kind eyes put me at ease. "You should hear some of the phrases that come out of my brother's mouth when he's here. I assure you none of them are accidental."

My eyes widen. It has been quite some time since any photographs of him have shown up in newspapers or magazines, but I recognize him now.

"You're Prince Benedict," I say, but he shakes his head.

"I prefer Father Benedict, if that's okay with you, Miss—"

"Kate," I say, extending a hand. Though I'm not sure that's the appropriate gesture. He obliges me nonetheless.

"The matchmaker, I presume?"

I swallow. "How did you know?"

"Come," he says, nodding toward the exit. "It's such a beautiful morning. Let us sit in the sun."

I follow him to a small garden where we settle on a stone bench. He tilts his head toward the sky and closes his eyes, breathing in the morning air.

"Has Nikolai spoken of me?" I ask, ashamed at my boldness, but I don't have time to beat around the bush.

Benedict folds his hands in his lap and simply nods.

"Do you truly care for my brother, Kate?"

My cheeks grow hot, and tears prick the backs of my eyes. I have not even told Nikolai of my feelings. Caring for him is not allowed. He is destined for another woman.

Benedict smiles again. "Your reaction is answer enough," he says. "So I will tell you two things. The first is that I love Nikolai, and I will do anything I can to protect him—and anything I can to help him find happiness, something I don't believe he's been capable of feeling for quite some time."

I swipe a finger under my eye, clearing away an escaping tear.

"The second is that if his happiness lies with someone who does not fit the parameters of the Royal Marriage Decree, I will do all that I can to find a way around it if Nikolai is ready to stop playing his games and fight for something real. Do you understand this, Miss Kate?"

I nod and fight the urge to hug him.

Nikolai and I have an ally. It is not a solution, but it is hope.

"Thank you," I whisper instead, but I grab his hand, pressing it between my own. "Thank you so much."

I decide not to overstay my welcome. I don't want to worry Nikolai if I'm gone too long. But as I'm walking away, Benedict calls after me.

"You may very well secure his heart," he says, and I pause midstep. "Just remember that if you do, it is not only yours to cherish, it is yours to protect."

I don't turn around or respond but instead continue on my way.

He knows I heard.

He knows I understand.

He knows Nikolai might just secure my heart, as well.

CHAPTER FOURTEEN

Nikolai

KATE RETURNS FROM her walk in a pensive mood.

"Everything okay, Pet?" I ask with no small concern. Her cheeks are white as marble.

She presses her lips into a grin, but it doesn't quite reach her eyes. So I make that my singular purpose for the hours ahead, to wash away whatever plagues her and get her beautiful blue eyes to smile again.

Today is the sole day in the month when tourists flood the palace and our extensive grounds. Social media shall soon be filled with #royalday #palacelife #princenikolaiwhereareyou #princenikolaihereicome posts.

And the women who flock inside aren't lying.

Invariably, a few overenthusiastic subjects attempt to break into my royal suite. Once, a coed from the University of Edenvale evaded the guards and made it all the way to my door wearing nothing but a yellow rain slicker and a pair of Wellingtons. Luckily, X was brushing up on his Japanese ninja star throwing skills in the antechamber off my residence, and the sight of him clutching a deadly iron *shuriken* halted her explorations and sent her fleeing for friendlier environments.

But today, I don't want to mix among my subjects. Nor do I want the public world to have a peek at the intimacy developing between me and Kate. All I want is to whisk her somewhere far away from prying eyes, and thanks to my helicopter, this is an entirely plausible option.

"I have a surprise," I tell her, picking up a woven brown picnic basket. X would normally be happy to carry such items, but I want this date to be all from me. For the next few hours there won't be any sign of bad boy Prince Nikolai putting his signature moves on a woman. Instead, she will be with a man who is taking a wonderful woman to a place that couldn't match her vibrant beauty, but comes close.

"We're having a picnic?"

"I made the sandwiches myself…and got lost trying to find the palace kitchen," I admit with a rueful grin.

She giggles, half in horror and half in amusement. "Please tell me you are joking."

I shrug. "In my world, you ring a silver bell, and whatever you need appears."

She stares at me with her signature intense gaze for long enough that my heart pounds. Does she see me as nothing more than a spoiled, overgrown brat?

"So if you tinkle your little bell, your wishes all come true."

I nod. "The palace staff pride themselves on this point."

She glances around the room. "Would this magic bell work for me?"

A thought scuttles through my brain like a menacing cockroach. *Does she value your worth more than you?* I stomp the passing notion into a million unrecognizable pieces. This is Kate. She isn't a gold digger. She could never be. "But of course. It's there on the table, beside the chaise lounge."

She eyes it and gives her chin a musing rub. "What if I ring for Hugh Jackman? The Wolverine version."

I choke on my breath, coughing into my fist.

"What can I say?" She stares with wide-eyed innocence. "I like my men with a sharp edge."

I cross the room, settle my hands on her hips to pull her as close as possible to me and my rapidly thickening needs. "You want me to snarl?"

"Maybe," she says, her voice lilting, teasing, driving me mad.

"You are playing with fire, Pet."

She nods. "Are you saying that I make you burn?" She rocks herself against me with a wink.

I nearly groan aloud. "Come, before I ravish you here and waste all these Nutella sandwiches."

She claps her hands. "You made *Nutella* sandwiches?"

I grin. "With bananas from Hawaii sliced over sourdough imported from San Francisco."

Her eyes brighten, finally, and the sight of her unencumbered joy makes my heart race.

"Nutella sandwiches with banana are my favorite. How did you know?"

"I may or may not have perused your Facebook account. You don't post often. I was hoping for a few more selfies."

Her mouth makes a perfect O, utterly adorable and unassumingly sexy as hell.

"The profile *About Me* section says…" I clear my throat. "'The quickest way to my heart is through a Nutella sandwich.'"

"Guilty as charged," she says with a giggle. "If you read the rest, you'd see it says you'd capture my heart forever if you added bananas." She raises a brow.

"Does it now?" I ask, and she merely shrugs.

We start to walk before I hold up a hand. "Wait, I need to get you something." I open the hallway closet door and pull out two hangers, one with a brand-new sundress and another with one of my jackets. "X procured you fresh garments for our journey, and I want to make sure you don't get cold on the way."

She smiles at the floral printed dress, but her brows knit together when I hand her the jacket. "You're planning on blasting the air-conditioning in the Rolls?"

I click my tongue. "No, we'll be flying at ten thousand feet." I smile into her uncomprehending face. "We're taking my helicopter to a little place I know." I lean over to kiss her forehead. "Me, you and the most beautiful place on Earth. What can go wrong?"

Kate

Nikolai fastens my seat belt and affixes the helmet strap.

"Are you shaking, Pet?" he asks, planting the sweetest of kisses on my nose.

I inhale a trembling breath. "I guess now wouldn't be the *best* time to tell you I've never flown before?"

He grins. "In a helicopter, you mean."

I shake my head. "I've never gone farther than a train could take me, and even then I never left the outskirts of Edenvale," I tell him, almost ashamed of my words. My fiancé was the adventurer, but he always took that to the extreme. It was never my desire to join him. Plus, Gran's health has been declining for years. "I don't know," I say, not wanting to burst Nikolai's bubble of excitement. Then I shrug. "I guess I'm the kind of girl who plays it safe."

Until I let my country's future king pleasure me in the royal gardens.

My head spins. My world is so small compared to his, and each revelation of my upbringing must remind him of this.

He rests his hands on my hips, so strong and reassuring. And as ridiculous as I must look in this helmet, he kisses me, his lips a promise that he will keep me safe.

"I want to show you so much," he whispers against me. "I want to give you the world."

I suck in a sharp breath. "I want that, too," I tell him. And with one more kiss, he hops from my side of the helicopter and makes his way to his own.

His helmet on and seat belt fastened, he flips a few switches and grips what looks like a very complicated gearshift. And then my stomach plummets from my body and probably through the cockpit floor as the ground drops out from under us.

I yelp.

"Shit. Are you okay?"

Concern laces Nikolai's voice as it pipes through the small speakers close to my ears. It's then that I start giggling.

"This…is…amazing!" I squeal as the palace shrinks beneath us—as all of Edenvale, the only home I've ever known, begins to disappear. I turn to him, eyes wide in amazement. *"Nikolai."*

He nods. "I know, Pet. I know."

We rise above mountains and valleys. The outskirts of our country's rolling green hills spread out before us like an emerald blanket.

"Grab the cyclic," he says, nodding toward the joystick next to my leg.

I shake my head violently.

"Don't worry. I won't let us fall."

I swallow and do as he says. He flips another couple of switches and then grins at me.

"Now—tilt it ever so slightly to the right."

I do it, my hands shaking yet gentle on what will either fly us in the direction he wants or be the instrument of our doom. To my surprise, the helicopter veers right, and I squeal with delight.

"I'm flying it!" I cry.

"You're flying it, Kate."

My heart surges at his utterance of my name. Though I enjoy his term of endearment, something about him calling me *Kate* makes whatever today is all the more real.

Nearly two hours later we land in an open field that is lusher and greener than any I've seen. Nikolai leads me several yards away to a country road, a motorbike parked on the gravel beside it.

"How did you—?" I start, and Nikolai answers me with a kiss so deep and full of need that my knees buckle.

"Careful there, Pet. The day's only just begun."

My grandmother, I think, the real world intruding

on the fantasy about to begin. "Nikolai, I need to get back—"

He kisses my nose. "Let go of home, if only for today. I promise to get you back to your life…and me back to mine." There is regret in his tone. "Just give me this day."

I nod and swallow back the threat of tears.

He fastens the picnic basket to the back of the bike and once again fastens a helmet to my head. He helps me onto the seat and then hops on in front of me.

"Don't let go," he says as I wrap my arms around his waist, and I squeeze him tight, my silent promise to obey.

The hills we ride are bumpy, on the verge of treacherous at times as we wind through the mountains. Nikolai has not told me where we are, but when we arrive at our destination, I know without the day having really begun that it will be the best one of my life.

"Nikolai," I say again as he helps me off the motorbike. I open my mouth to say more, but tears prick at my eyes, and I am left speechless, staring out over white rocks and turquoise water, a small bathing pool with a cascading waterfall at its end.

He removes his helmet and then my own as I continue to gape at the site before me.

"I wanted to bring you somewhere as beautiful as you," he says. "Such a place doesn't exist, but I do believe this is the closest I'll get."

This time I'm powerless against the few tears that fall. I don't recall knowing happiness like this.

He pulls the basket from the bike and then lifts a small hatch beneath the basket's perch, pulling out a pair of socks and hiking boots.

I laugh as I look at my ballet flats. Sensible shoes, yet not sensible enough for the terrain we are about to traipse.

"Your glass slippers, Cinderella," he says, and I lean against the vehicle, allowing him to lace me into the boots. On the second one, his hands travel up the length of my leg, and his lips trail sweet kisses in their wake.

I give his head a playful tap. "Not until I get my Nutella sandwich," I say, though if he truly wanted to, he could have me right here on the side of the road.

We make our way to the pool, and Nikolai spreads a blanket upon an embankment.

"Are we the only ones here?" I ask. "And by the way, *where* is here?"

He retrieves a sandwich from the basket, removes it from its parchment wrapper and tears off a small piece.

"We are in the secluded hills of western Rosegate." He pops the sandwich bite into my mouth, and I hum my approval as chocolate, hazelnut and banana converge upon my tongue. "And I can assure you that *no one* will be visiting this pool today."

I swallow. "How—how deep is it?" I ask, and Nikolai's eyes soften.

"Not more than four feet, even at the deepest end. We don't have to go in. I knew you might not want to, but I also knew I couldn't *not* show you this place."

I shake my head, wanting to be brave for him—to be brave for *me*. I've been in water before—willingly. I just don't remember knowing how to swim.

"You'll keep me safe?" I ask.

His hands cradle my cheeks. "God, yes, Kate. Of course. *Always.*"

His gray eyes bore into mine, and I know he's telling the truth. It's that last word, *always*, that seals the deal.

I back away from him and kick off my boots. Then I pull my dress over my head, revealing my one surprise for him today.

"Where—where are your undergarments?" he stammers, and I beckon for him with my index finger.

"You've already given me the world today. I wanted to give something to you." As he steps closer, I begin to unbutton his shirt. "I want to tell you something. I—I hadn't been with anyone else for a couple of years before you." I squeeze my eyes shut and wait for the embarrassment to subside. When I feel his fingertips caress my cheeks, I open them again to see nothing but pure adoration in his gaze. "I was engaged and—he died. I didn't say anything before because—"

"It's okay," he says, surprising me with his reassurance as his hand still cradles my face. "I guess we are more alike than we thought."

He means Victoria. And maybe he's right. Maybe our worlds aren't so far apart after all.

I nod. "What I'm trying to say is… I've been on birth control the whole time. Because it was easier… because I hoped that maybe someday…"

He grins. "I'm clean," he says, knowing what I'm trying to ask. "I may be a wicked rake much of the time, but I'm always careful. If you want to know how many times a year I get tested…"

I shake my head, deciding to trust him rather than wonder how the frequency of doctor's visits factors into the ratio of women he's been with.

"I want to *be* with you, Nikolai. Like this. If you want to be with me."

"There's only been one other I've been with—like this." He growls softly in my ear. "And there is *nothing* I want more right now."

So I free him of his clothes, marveling at his naked body—each ridge of his muscles, the black ink of his tattoos.

"Tell me what it means," I say, tracing the compass with my finger as I've done before.

He brings my hand to his lips, pressing a kiss into my palm.

"It means I was lost," he says. "But I'm not anymore."

I nod, unable to speak. So we step carefully from our perch, down the rocks and into the warm crystal waters below.

"Make love to me," I say, wrapping my arms around his neck, his hard cock already nudging me open. I am slick and ready—just from his words—to take him in.

He pushes inside, and I cry out as my legs wrap around his hips. I am weightless in the water. Weightless in his arms. Gravity no longer exists.

And I never, ever want to come back down.

CHAPTER FIFTEEN

Nikolai

MY COCK SHEATHES itself inside Kate, her intimate muscles clenching my length, and a single word hits like a punch to the soul. *Home.* I have traveled the world, set foot on every continent, skied sky-kissing alpine slopes, explored tiger-filled jungles and indulged in exclusive VIP sex clubs in most major cities, yet I've always felt adrift, empty, as if I live my life surrounded by an invisible moat.

Kate might never have set a single stiletto beyond our small kingdom's borders, but when we lock gazes, it is as if the whole fucking universe is in her eyes.

She is my home.

I withdraw, take my hard cock in one hand and press the tip to her clit, stroking her hot wet center in a slow, hip-grinding circle. This realization makes me dizzy. I knew she'd attracted me, then entranced me. But this feeling requires me to get out a thesaurus, search for superlatives. And yet it might be simple. So goddamn simple.

Her lips part as her pupils dilate.

"Good, Pet?" My voice is husky with emotion. I

want to make her come so hard that the memory of the pleasure imprints on her skin, engraves in her bones.

"Amazing, but…" She trails off, lowering her lids.

I smooth a strand of fiery hair from her cheek. "No secrets between us. No barriers. I am here, raw, skin to skin. I demand no less from you."

"I need you back inside me."

The urgency lacing her plea is almost my undoing. "Your wish is my command, m'lady."

I hike her off her feet and position her slender thighs around my hips. She tries to wiggle lower, but I hold her firmly as I begin my trek toward the waterfall.

"Please. Nikolai. In me. Now."

I intend to bury myself in her so deep that I no longer know where she ends and I begin. But first she needs her surprise.

We pass under the fall, and the intense pounding rush is nothing to the thundering pulse of my blood in my ears.

Inside the cave there is a small crack in the ceiling, and a shaft of perfect buttery sunlight sparkles over the crystal walls.

Kate gasps. "What is this magical place?"

I bury my face in her porcelain neck and breathe in her essence, the faint hint of Chanel No. 5. "The Grotto of Diamonds," I rumble. "Stunning, isn't it?"

Her chest heaves against me.

"Absolutely breathtaking," she says.

I cup her chin, refuse to let her grow demure, to be shy. "Wasn't talking about the grotto."

With a pump, I am back inside. Fucking Christ. My ass muscles clench. She feels softer than spun silk, tight, wet and perfect. As much as I want to lose myself in a series of punishing, dominating thrusts, this is for her. This day. This trip. This moment. So I take the time to ensure every stroke glides over her clit in the slow, steady rhythm that she craves. When I settle her ass against a smooth rock, she hisses with pleasure.

"There's a hot spring running down the wall here," I rasp.

She hums. "This feels amazing." The warm water seeps between her legs, splashing my own thighs.

She arches with pleasure like a naughty kitten and I slide the final inch. Fuck. Her pussy milks me in micropulses. Savage pleasure claws my chest. She is so close already. My darling Kate is responsive as hell. But I won't find my release until she gets hers.

I dip over her sensitive nipple and trace the rosy bud with the flat of my tongue while I enter her over and over, deeper and deeper. Her nails claw my back helplessly. Those micropulses become quakes.

"Watch me, Pet. Watch *us*. Watch your sweet pussy take all that I have to give."

We stare through the crystalline water, hypnotized at the erotic sight of my thick root working through her pink entrance. It's the most goddamn beautiful sight that has ever existed.

"This is where I belong," I say. "In you. Giving you everything you deserve."

"I love watching you take me," she gasps.

"Love watching you get it."

Then her dizzy gasp turns to a small cry. "It's so good. It's too much. I'm coming."

"And who is giving it to you?"

"Nikolai."

As she breathes my name I shoot inside her, my own

groan losing itself in her mouth as I taste the ecstasy on her tongue.

We spend the day like this. Lovemaking in the Grotto of Diamonds. Nibbling Nutella sandwiches. Sharing funny stories about our childhoods. Each moment is the best one of my life.

When at last I fly us home, she falls asleep in her seat, too satiated to fear the helicopter, and among the night sky, I tell the stars my secrets, the truth that's burning a hole in my heart. The one that I am not yet ready to confess to her face.

For now, the truth lies in the sky above—and buried deep within my long-darkened soul.

Kate

I feel his fingertips softly caress my face, and I stir in my seat. I'm vaguely aware of my surroundings—a helicopter, I think—but I don't want to leave the dream, one where Nikolai tells me he loves me.

"We're home, Pet. Time to wake."

His voice is soft in my ear, and my body betrays me as my eyes flutter open, exiting the fairy tale I so long to stay in. Because of course he never spoke those words, and I'm not the princess who gets her happily ever after. Yet after this day, I can't help but hope for the possibility that one day I will be.

The propeller blades are still, and Nikolai no longer wears his helmet. I reach a hand to my own head and find that neither do I.

"Wow," I say. "I was really out. What time is it?" It's only then that I realize the setting sun—that I remember Maddie spending the day at the hospital with Gran.

"It's nearly six," he says. "Is everything okay?"

I fling off my seat belt and fidget with the door. "I'm sorry. Today was—it was everything, but I'm late. It's a family thing. I—I have to go."

I must sound as frantic as I feel because he rushes from the helicopter and around to my side, helping me out.

"Whatever you need. Where do you have to go? I'll take you there myself."

We race from the helipad where I expect to see X waiting with the Rolls-Royce, but instead I find two guards along with Queen Adele. Christian Wurtzer. And a young woman I recognize from the covers of various magazines—Catriona Wurtzer. She stands with a self-satisfied grin plastered on her face and one hand distinctively rubbing her flat belly.

"What is all this?" Nikolai asks, more annoyed than concerned.

Christian's jaw is tight, and I can tell he is using monumental restraint. Whatever is going on, this man looks at Nikolai like he wants to tear his throat out.

The queen purses her lips and narrows her eyes at me. "Come now, Nikolai. Really. Dallying with the hired *help*. I'd like to know how she plans to earn double her fee for getting you down the aisle if she can't keep her legs crossed in your presence." She sets her cold gaze on me. "And *you*." The queen raises her brows. "I know I told you to earn his trust, but I had no idea you'd seduce him, as well. I guess that *is* one way to go about it."

Her lips part into a satisfied, victorious grin.

"Double fee? What the fuck is this about a double fee?" Nikolai asks.

The world seems to spin around me. I might be sick.

Christian's jaw ticks. Catriona stifles a laugh. And when I look at Nikolai, the light in his eyes snuffs out as I watch his gaze cool and then turn completely to ice.

"Double your fee?" he repeats, his tone achingly bitter.

"The contract," I say, but it comes out as a strangled sob. "You have the copy. The money wasn't a secret." But he told me he hadn't read it, which means I let the lie of omission stand. I let myself believe that what he didn't know wouldn't hurt him. I let myself believe that we could beat the queen at her own game, but I never really stood a chance. Did I?

"I trusted you," he says. "But I guess that was just part of your job too. I didn't think I needed a contract to prove to me that you weren't like every other woman who's schemed to get in my bed. If it wasn't meant to be kept from me, then why not say something?" he asks, his words biting and bitter. "Is this why you challenged me? Why you were so confident you'd succeed? Because you were allied with the person who despises me most?"

He steps toward me, his face inches from mine, but I don't for one second think he will kiss me, not with his teeth clenched. Or that vein in his neck throbbing with the hot anger rising from his body.

"Was. Any. Of. It. Real?"

Each word stabs me like a poisoned dagger.

"Nikolai, you *know* it was real," I say, but how can he trust me now when the queen speaks the truth? She didn't request my help. She demanded it, under veiled threats. I *was* her ally. I had no choice but to comply. And even though I gained his trust, I never really gave him mine. Or I'd have been brave enough to tell him everything.

I knew I was falling for him today, and the possibility of us made me think I wasn't afraid of her anymore—that I could tell Nikolai about Gran. About why I needed to succeed even if it meant breaking my own heart.

She played me. She played him. And now she is going to win.

"Money," he says, his voice so distant I almost don't believe it's the same man who woke me moments ago. "That's what you really hoped to gain. Wasn't it?"

I shake my head, refusing to believe things can change with one utterance from the queen. "You know that's not true. She *made* me agree. I had no choice. I should have told you everything, but that doesn't mean—"

"Stop," he says. "Just stop. Why would you say anything if *seducing* me could earn you double your fee?" His eyes flash to the queen and back to me. "Do you want to know why I refuse to marry?" he asks, but he doesn't wait for an answer. "Because the last woman I asked to be my queen was willing to accept my hand even though she loved another. All because she thought the title more important than all else. Now she is gone, my brother banished, and I right back where I started, fooling myself that any woman could see past the facade."

He takes another step closer to me, and I flinch. I do not know this Nikolai. *This* is not my prince.

"I told you. I will. Not. Marry."

Laughter bubbles from the queen's lips, and she claps her hands slowly.

"Lovely speech. Really. Lovely. But here is the thing. It was only a matter of time before your—dalliances— got you into trouble. Thankfully, the countless times you've *dallied* with the baroness seem to have worked in your favor." Her lips curled into a malicious grin. "Catriona is pregnant with your heir. You *will* marry and secure an alliance with Rosegate…or lose the throne."

Nikolai's eyes widen as his gaze meets that of his former lover, and then falls to where her hand rests on her belly.

My tears fall hot and fast because I know now we never had a chance—Nikolai and I. The queen had said she would find his match and that I would support it. Benedict searching for a loophole was nothing more than a distraction. This was always going to end.

"Take her away until I decide what to do with her," the queen says.

And before I can comprehend that she means me, both of her guards appear at my sides, my arms firm in their grip.

"What are you doing?" I cry.

"Your Highness," Christian starts. "You never said anything about locking her up!"

But the queen waves him off.

"Take. Her. Away," she says again, and the guards start dragging me toward a car at the edge of the grounds.

"Nikolai!" I call. "Listen to me. You know it was never about the money. I know you do."

But he doesn't respond as the guards pull me farther and farther from him.

I want to cry out again, but for whom? Nikolai stands there, dumbfounded and shattered. I have no ally.

As I collapse into the back of the car, my eyes blur

with tears—so much so that it takes me several seconds to get my bearings.

A minibar. A bottle of cognac. And when I look up, the window between me and the driver lowers.

"To the dungeon, then, Miss?" the driver asks, and I dare to let myself hope.

"X?"

CHAPTER SIXTEEN

Nikolai

"Tsk, tsk." Adele clicks her tongue. Her mouth's sympathetic purse only serves to make the triumph in her eyes more grotesque. Not for the first time I wonder just how she managed to capture my father's heart. She hails from an old Edenvale family, aristocratic to the core, but besmirched by a long line of traitors who over time have betrayed our throne's integrity to cut lucrative deals with Nightgardin, hoping to profit in the destabilization. A few of her ancestors' heads decorated the palace bridge as a warning to other transgressors.

I flex my fist, wishing for an ancient ax and a chopping block.

"Naughty, naughty, Nikolai, leading that pathetic matchmaker on. I hope you had fun with your little game. I'm sure she'll get over it in, oh, ten or twenty years." She glances to Catriona, and they share the same tinkling, malevolent laugh.

I don't know what the fuck to think. Two hours ago I was making love to a woman who I'd have sworn looked into my pitch-black soul and saw a man worthy of her heart. Now I'm being told it was a lie? That she was in it for a double fee. It's not even the money that gets me this time. It's that she kept her alliance with the queen rather than me. I've been enough of a royal idiot to be duped into thinking Kate had grown to care for me for my own sake.

Idiot.

Self-disgust roils through me. But I don't allow a trace of feeling to reveal itself on my face.

Instead, I twist my own lips into a sneer. "Pity." I ensure my words are ice, that they drip with scorn. "For a commoner, she was uncommon good fun." I allow my gaze to fall on Catriona. Her white-blond hair. Her porcelain perfect skin and pale blue eyes nearly the same shade of water. Nothing warm or welcoming. No. Twin pools of an Arctic lake. I take my time scanning every inch of her perfect body. "Darling," I drawl. "You didn't need to fake a pregnancy to keep my interest. The way I recall, we have unfinished business. You promised me a backstage pass and never delivered." I arch a brow.

"You bastard," Christian says, lunging for me. The two guards, already returned, restrain him.

"I think you meant to say Your Highness." I dust off my shirtfront. "I do believe the proper terminology in addressing your liege lord is Sire, Prince, Majesty. You could go for Your Most Exalted Worshipfulness for extra credit. You always were an ass kisser back in school."

And he was. Perfect grades. Awards for chivalry. While my extracurricular activities consisted of fucking Miss Teatree, the student French teacher, in the back of my Rolls-Royce during lunch breaks.

"I am going to cut out your disgusting tongue," he hisses.

"Your loyalty to your sister is commendable," I answer easily. "But problematic. Because either she is lying, in which case you are a fool, or she is telling the truth, and you are threatening violence not only on your future king but also the father of your nephew. A child who will be the only one to carry on your noble line given your…dilemma."

Christian stares at me with fire in his eyes. He contracted mumps during our school days, and the nurse told him he was probably sterile. A pity as it puts his small but highly coveted territory in jeopardy. Rosegate needs an heir. Edenvale needs to solidify the alliance. Despite the circumstances, it would be an advantageous match.

"My money is that you are a fool," I say, turning back to Catriona. "How do you know that you are pregnant? Will you have me believe you are some sort of modern-day Princess and the Pea? That you can magically sense if my child is growing within you?"

"Don't be ridiculous," Adele snaps, beckoning to a butler who stands off to the side, holding a silver platter covered by a swan-shaped lid.

He hurries over and removes the lid with a flourishing bow. On the tray lies a pregnancy stick with two lines.

"I do not read hieroglyphics," I mumble.

"Idiocy doesn't become you. It's obvious that's a positive sign." Victory is stamped on my stepmother's every smug feature. "You coated her womb with your depraved seed. Time to do your duty."

"A little baby," Catriona says, her mouth curving into an uncertain smile. "A future king or queen. Plus, Rosegate will unite with Edenvale at last, and Nightgardin won't ever have a chance of taking it over."

My stepmother inclines her head as if truer words had never been spoken. What is her poisonous endgame? I have to think, but my brain is flatlining, my neurons only able to process one thing. That I let another woman pretend to care for me. That I let down my defenses and gave Kate entry into my inner keep.

My stepmother hates me, blames me for her daughter's death, but why the fuck is she so intent on marrying me off to Catriona, or marrying me off period? I am not buying her giving a flying fuck over solidifying ties to Rosegate.

The cogs in my dulled brain begin to creak back to life. Doubt slides up my spine like a serpent. I used condoms with Catriona. She said she was also on birth control. If Kate was working with Adele, why not Catriona, too?

If it looks like a duck and quacks like a duck…

"The wedding will be in three days' time," Adele says. "A very private, very legally binding ceremony."

The queen might be crafty, but she isn't exactly a rocket scientist. And about as subtle as a doorpost.

"I don't think so." It takes all my strength not to gnash my teeth. "I know I've been nothing but a crushing disappointment to your selfish motives, so just add this latest mistake to my tab."

I turn away, thoughts reeling. If Catriona is carrying my child, I can't abandon her or the innocent baby, but I can't marry her. I'll order a blood test and then figure things out. Even if the ache of betrayal floods my body as I think of the woman who just disappeared into the night, I know it was real for me, so much so that I can barely breathe thinking it was all a game for her. I want to fall to my knees and scream. I want to find a wall and punch it until my fists run with blood.

Love is my curse, never my salvation. When Father dies, I will sit on the Stone Throne, but my heart will be as impenetrable as a block of uncut granite. Perhaps Catriona will bear my bastard, but she will never be my queen.

X. I need X. He'll know what to do. Even if it is to get me mind-numbingly drunk until today is blacked out of memory—he'll know.

"I will make you happy," Catriona says, putting the perfect quaver in her voice. She's such a drama queen that I'm half tempted to give her access to the throne, just to watch the spectacle.

"Sweetheart, there is only one reason why I stuck my dick in you. Fine, two. But the primary reason was this… I was trying to find out if your brother was selling me out to the tabloids again."

"What are you bloody talking about?" Christian yells.

"Every time I went out in the past year, images would appear of me online and in the print media. Despite my reputation, I do value discretion when it suits me. I knew someone in my entourage was spilling the proverbial beans. Squeaking to the press. But it was you all along. You were the little mouse." I'm unleashing the asshole attitude that's made me infamous, going full scale royal prick.

There is no one that I can trust. I am as I have always been—alone.

Catriona presses a hand to her heart. "How could you accuse me of such base behavior?"

My shoulders shake with my cold laugh. "The minute Christian found me with you, I knew it wasn't him. He was so upset. Then nothing leaked afterward. Except there was an attempt to sell something to a national magazine, wasn't there?"

She blanches. If she was pale before, now Catriona is a living ghost.

"X intercepted the messages. You were going to sell a tell-all exposé to the highest bidder. Did you think that texting your brother to come find you in my bed was going to force him to badger me to marry you? Or that you'd achieve notoriety as my lover?"

Catriona draws her hand back and slaps me hard on the cheek. "You are a monster. No wonder Victoria ran off with Damien. You can't love. Your heart is complete and utter stone."

"Enough!" Adele commands in her usual imperious tone. "Someone escort my sniveling future daughter-in-law back inside the palace. And her brother, before he murders the heir to the throne."

The crowd clears, and within minutes it's just my stepmother and me.

"Why are you doing this?" I ask at last, breaking the silence. No more pretense. I just want answers.

"I've waited for this moment a long time," she purrs. "Ever since I buried my daughter in the cold, hard ground."

And I believe her. I just don't believe that is the

whole truth. But do I trust this inner voice, the same intuition that whispered that I should take a chance on Kate? The one that has led me back here, to this black place of pain and bone-crushing loneliness? Victoria hurt my heart. Kate detonated it with the precision of a lobbed grenade. It will never be whole.

As I begin to search for answers, one truth is certain. Not only will I never marry, I will never love again.

Kate

A heavy gated door scrapes across stone as it slams shut behind me. I stumble into the cold, dank cell and stare with wide eyes back at the man who just threw me in here.

"X," I say, my voice shaking. "Why?"

He stares at me without expression, and my fear starts to morph into something fierce. I throw myself at the bars separating me from him, shaking them to no avail.

"I care about him—so much! You know I do."

My heart beats wildly in my chest. I can't even say it to X, that I *love* Nikolai. But he watched me get carted away thinking I betrayed him because I was too afraid to tell him the truth.

Because I'm a fool to have ever thought I could bridge the divide between his world and mine.

"This—this is all the queen," I continue. "She told me she would choose his bride, that if I didn't comply my sister's business would be ruined. You know she has the power to do that. You know she set this whole thing up!"

Still he stands, arms crossed, impassive as ever.

I pace, shivering in the damp air, tears pouring along my cheeks. When X says nothing, I collapse onto a stone bench at the rear of the cell and let out a bitter laugh.

"I didn't think places like this were real, you know. Castles? Sure. But dungeons? This is the stuff of fairy tales," I tell my emotionless captor. "But I never expected to be the princess. I only ever wanted to take care of my family."

I meet X's stare. There is no sign that he's even heard a word I've said, yet I swear I see a twinkle in his eyes that wasn't there before.

"The money?" I say, my voice steady now because even if Nikolai won't hear me out, he will know the truth. "My sister and I live and work out of our small apartment. Every cent that doesn't go toward our monthly payments, toward food or keeping the business afloat—it goes to the elderly care center where our grandmother lives. And now it will go to the hospital that's keeping her alive. That's where I'm supposed to be now, X. *Please.* Let me go to her."

X's jaw tightens, the only sign that any of this is getting through to him.

I open my mouth to say something more but am interrupted by what sounds like a sack of potatoes hitting the stone floor.

X looks to his left, and his features finally relax.

"You have three minutes to decide if you trust me,

Miss Kate. Three minutes to decide if you are willing to put your life in my hands."

I rise from the stone bench and make my way to the iron gate that separates me from him, pressing my face against the bars so I can see what X sees—a burly palace guard slumped on the floor next to a stool, an empty beer stein tipped over next to him.

"Yes, I drugged his ale." X waves a hand. "It won't be the first time he's fallen asleep on watch, but it is the first time it's of my doing. He'll be lucky not to piss himself with relief when he wakes to find he hasn't been caught."

The corner of his mouth quirks ever so slightly into the hint of a grin, and my heart surges with hope.

"You don't need to prove your love, Kate. Not to me," he says, his voice a firm whisper. And just like Nikolai calling me Kate somehow made me know that what we had was real, X doing the same—dropping that ridiculous *Miss*—tells me I can trust him, too.

"I've known of your family's situation since the king and queen hired you," he goes on. "But the prince—he has been in the dark, and you are one of those responsible for keeping him there."

My breath hitches, and I swallow back a sob. He is right. Nikolai hid nothing from me, but I hid my life from him. Even if it was for my own protection, I betrayed his trust in doing so.

I nod. "This isn't my world," I tell him. "I'm out of my depth. And as much as he means to me—as much as my silly secret wish has been for him to choose *me*—I knew it was a fool's errand to think he could ever truly be mine. I must think about my family right now. And Nikolai—" I stutter on the next thought, but it is the only way. "Nikolai must marry Catriona. If she's carrying his baby, he must." I swallow hard against the ache in my chest, against the cavern that will replace my heart after my next words. "Tell the queen I forfeit my fee. Tell *Nikolai*. I will not cause trouble for the prince. I just need to get to my family."

X nods somberly at me. "Queen Adele plans to leave you here until after the wedding." My whole body begins to shake as his words sink in.

Another tear slides down my cheek. "When will that be?" I ask.

X clears his throat. "Three days' time," he says. "I hope you understand I *had* to bring you here. The prince's safety depends on it."

I glance around my cell and shudder not just at the thought of being locked here for three days or of losing Nikolai—but that such cruelty exists in the queen's heart.

"Father Benedict is working tirelessly to find a loophole," X continues. "If this baby is not Nikolai's—and if there is a way out of the decree—he will find it within these three days. If I let you go, though," he says, "the queen will expedite the wedding, and Nikolai will have no chance at true happiness. But if you trust me—if you trust that my one and only mission is to protect my prince—then you can leave here tonight."

I wipe the tears from my face, my hands now covered in dirt from the filthy cell bars. I'm sure I look as frightened as I feel, but I don't care. I don't care about anything but protecting my family and the man that I love, even if he will never know my true feelings.

Everything inside me trembles so hard I fear my bones will shatter. But I hold my head high and look straight into X's unwavering stare.

"I trust you," I say. "For Maddie. For my grandmother. For Nikolai, all whom I love. I trust you, X."

He pulls a small vial from his coat pocket and hands it to me through the bars.

"Then drink."

CHAPTER SEVENTEEN

Nikolai

"WALK WITH ME." Adele gathers her crimson skirts and strides toward the gloomy entrance to the maze.

I follow as if in a trance. My head pounds, and my brain is reeling. Too many questions. Too many years living with lies and pain and never knowing who to trust. Who, if anyone has, ever loved me for me?

Maybe no one.

A feeling of utter loneliness swallows me.

Do I want to be king? It's never been a question that I've consciously asked myself before. It's as inevitable as drawing a breath. The next beat of my heart. Someday I will sit on the Stone Throne in the Reception Hall and lead my people into what I have always hoped in my deepest heart would be a prosperous and bright future.

But I don't want to be king at this price. My birthright isn't worth letting Adele win at her twisted game. But I don't know the rules. I don't know how to beat her when she holds all the cards. But the worst thing that can happen is to let her sense my uncertainty. That would be like slicing my wrists in a shark tank. Better to square my shoulders, set my jaw and figure this the fuck out. She will make a mistake. I just need to stay sharp, be ready to pounce at the first misstep.

"So quiet, no? As if the world holds its collective breath." Adele runs her fingers over the hedgerow. "Why the long face? I'd think you would enjoy taking a stroll down memory lane." Her voice is steeped in innuendo.

I ball my hands into tight fists. "I don't know what you are talking about."

"Now, now. Coy's not a good look on you, Nikolai," she croons. "We might *dislike* each other, but do let's be frank. I know how you ravished the lovely Kate Winter here on the ground of the maze. You feasted and rutted on her with your face like the wild beast that you are, depraved by lust. Disgusting and yet fascinating."

I stare at her, blinking slowly.

"How do I know your...*activities*?" She leers. "Please. You think your father runs this place? Why do you think I encourage all of his travels for diplomacy? This is *my* kingdom, and I have eyes *everywhere*." She enunciates each syllable of that last word. "A mouse doesn't so much as shit in this palace without me getting an update." She shakes her head in mock sorrow. "Now don't get all pouty. No one likes a sore loser." Her eyes gleam. "And you've lost, my sweet prince. You have lost so much that I'd be tempted to pity you if I wasn't so absolutely delighted."

Her laugh cuts my skin like glass shards before it morphs into a hysterical sob. "My daughter should have been queen!" she snaps. "It was *her* destiny to save Rosegate, not that dimwit Catriona."

My jaw clenches. "I *loved* Victoria." I choke out the

bitter truth. "But she was sleeping with my traitor of a brother."

She scoffs, sneering as she looks me up and down. "You are unfit to be king. A real man worries about affairs of the state, not of the heart. You are nothing but a weak fool. So what if Victoria didn't love you? She would have bedded you, born you an heir. She knew her duty. And your duty was to keep her safe! There were greater plans at work."

Every cell in my body recoils. "Wouldn't you want more for your daughter than to serve as a broodmare to a man she didn't love?"

"I wanted her to be queen," she hisses. "And to… and to… It doesn't matter! There is no more worthy goal than the pursuit of power. *You* took that away from her. And now I get to take your happiness from you."

Bile rises in my throat. "She loved my brother! *He* took her life, Adele. And he's been paying the price for years." An unexpected twinge of sympathy pierces me. I loved Victoria and lost her. Damien loved her and lost everything. I will not forgive my youngest brother, but only now when I have lost Kate—when I stand to lose everything if Adele has her way—do I have the slightest idea what life might be like to be banished.

"Damien was third in line to the throne." She speaks so forcefully spittle flies from her mouth. "You ran her off so she could be what? An insignificant nobody? Do you know who my family is, that we are a bloodline even more ancient than yours?"

I swipe my cheek, not having the slightest interest in getting into a snobby pissing match over who is the most royal. "I ran them both off after discovering them fucking like dogs in the Royal Library. And do you know what I think? I think she wanted me to catch her. I think she wanted me to *free* her from a future she never wanted as much as you did."

My chest heaves. I have to squeeze my eyes shut as the memory takes hold. It's not as if I don't hold some of the guilt. For years I've wondered if it could have gone differently. If there was something I could have done that would have set in motion a different course of events that did not end with Victoria dead. But the fact remains that she loved another, that she betrayed me and was all too happy to leave once she was caught.

"She'd still be alive if it wasn't for you." Adele flies at me, claws outstretched, grief taking her to the point of insanity.

This is my moment.

I've been waiting for a misstep. If she was playing a political game, her feelings for Victoria, the grief at losing not only a daughter but also a future meal ticket, muddles her thinking. She isn't calculating now. She is ready to tear me apart limb from limb, unleash her long-simmering resentment, the fact that she has had to kowtow to the Lorentz family to wear the crown, and now the best she will ever get is a puppet in Catriona, a weak-minded, selfish woman easily manipulated to do her bidding.

As for me, I'm ready to go to hell and bring Adele along for the ride. I am at the brink of endurance, and below me lies the bleak roiling blackness, the void that is there, always there. I'm done resisting. I'm ready to give myself over to the void.

She is right.

I've lost.

I've lost everything that matters.

The world goes crimson before a strong steady hand clamps my shoulder.

"Sire," X says in a grave voice, pulling me back. "Come quick. There is no time."

Kate

You will be able to hear all too clearly but see nothing. You'll feel the touch of others all too keenly but will be paralyzed from any movement yourself. You will be alive, but to anyone without sharp medical training, you will appear dead. Heartbeat too slow to detect, breathing too shallow to recognize.

This is what X tells me before I drink. There isn't time to ask him how he knows of such a drug or if he's seen it work before. I have mere seconds to decide that I trust him before everything goes black and I lose myself completely.

I feel the cold stone beneath my cheek but see nothing at all. I hear the frantic scuffle of shoes in the distance. The sound grows louder, and then there is nothing but silence for several long moments before the unmistakable click-clack of high heels approach.

"She was delirious. Screaming nonsense about how the queen threatened her livelihood if she did not get you down the aisle. Of course it was all rubbish," X says. "After her tirade she complained of shortness of breath. I knew she was just looking for a way out, so I ignored her pleas. And then she just—collapsed."

Metal clangs, and I swear the ground beneath me shakes.

"You *ignored* her?" His voice is hoarse, frantic, and I can feel his pain. It is as tangible as the stone against my cheek.

Nikolai! I want to cry out his name, but I'm stuck in this blackness, forced to do nothing but listen and to trust that I will be out of here soon.

"You bastard!" he growls, his voice wild. "I will kill you, X. I will fucking kill you!"

Laughter trills through Nikolai's madness. The queen. They are all here, staring at my prone body. And Nikolai thinks— Oh God. X. What have we done to him?

"Oh, this is too good," Adele says. "Not even in the plan, but it certainly makes things much easier for me. Tell me, X. Is she dead?"

"Unlock the fucking cell!" Nikolai bellows, interrupting her question.

"Oh, very well," the queen concedes. "Have your last look if you must."

Metal grates over stone, and I feel the faint warmth of skin against my own.

"There is no pulse," X says gravely. "Sire, my deepest condolences."

I hear a sickening crack and then Nikolai's broken voice. "I *will* kill you for this," he says again, and I'm not sure if he's speaking to the queen, or X, or both.

The scraping of heels comes nearer, and icy fingers touch my neck. If I wasn't already paralyzed, the queen's cold touch would do it.

"You didn't actually think I'd trust your word, X.

Did you? But it looks as if you're being truthful. The girl is dead."

Her skin leaves mine, and I fight to claw my way out of my body, out of this cell and away from her even though I know there's nothing more she can do to me—so long as she thinks I'm gone.

Seconds later I am weightless. No, I'm in someone's arms. I feel warm liquid splash on my cheek and know that it is my prince who cradles me.

"I'm so sorry," he whispers, and I feel his trembling lips press against my forehead. "I believe you," he whispers. "I trusted you, and I know in my gut it was the right thing to do, but I let the goddamn past get the better of me. I will never forgive myself for doubting you. I don't deserve your love, but I know you gave it to me today. I let my fear blind me to the truth, but know this, Kate. I love you. And I promise you this—I will *not* love another." And then in a voice so soft I almost miss it, I hear, "I win our wager," he says, his whisper cracking on that last word. "I will not marry—not if it means the woman beside me is not you. You owe me a favor, Kate. Those were our terms." I hear him take a shuddering breath. "Please. Come back."

My body rocks in his arms. Again and again warm drops of liquid splatter my cheek, and my heart cracks wide-open for the broken man who holds me. "Come back, Kate," he pleads, louder this time, and then his lips are on mine.

I taste the salt of his tears, and if I wasn't sure that I was, in fact, paralyzed, I would swear that my eyes leaked tears of their own. Kiss after soft kiss, he doesn't let go of me, not even when the queen groans.

"Enough already," she hisses. "You'll never know

loss like I do, Nikolai. But now you will live with yours
for a lifetime. Now, X. Wipe the blood from your lip
and do something with Miss Winter's body. I'm sure
you can conjure a reasonable explanation for the Royal
Guard, and I trust it will be kept from the papers."

"Yes, Your Highness," I hear X say.

I feel Nikolai lift my palm to his cheek, and my fingers twitch against his tear-soaked skin.

A throat clears. "Your Highness," X says, "is the
king not arriving back at the palace shortly? Surely
you want to be the first to break the news about the
prince and Catriona. I will—take care of things here."

"Yes. Fine," she says. "Nikolai, clean yourself up
and join us in the grand dining hall for dinner. You can
announce your impending nuptials yourself."

Nikolai says nothing, only holds my palm flat against
his cheek as I listen to the piercing blows of her heels
against the stone until the sound grows farther and farther away. Finally, I hear the far-off clank of the heavy
cellar door closing.

Nikolai lets go of my hand, but it doesn't fall. My
fingers twitch against his skin again, and I hear a sharp
intake of breath.

"X?" He draws out his servant's name.

"Really, Sire," X says, the slightest admonishment
in his voice, "I thought you had more faith in me than
that."

My eyes flutter open, and Nikolai's head is turned
toward the man who hopefully saved us both. I gasp as
my sluggish lungs gulp at the air while my heartbeat
feels like it's increasing at an exponential rate.

Both of their heads snap toward mine. X stares at
me with a satisfied grin on his face despite a split lower

lip. It's the first genuine smile I've seen from him, and I can't help but feel the slightest bit victorious. I vowed to make the man smile, and I did, even if I had to nearly die to do it.

Nikolai still holds me, his eyes wide and red rimmed.

I regain movement in my other arm and cradle his face in my palms.

"I *love* you, Nikolai," I say, my thumb swiping at a remaining tear on his cheek. "The money was never—"

But his lips are on mine before I get a chance to explain, and that's when I realize that I don't have to. He trusts that my love is real, and it is. God, it is. He pulls me closer, deepening the kiss as my lips part for him. My limbs are still weak, but he holds me so tight I know I won't fall.

"Sire," X interrupts. "We don't have much time. The drug was supposed to last longer. Perhaps I measured incorrectly in my haste. We must get Miss Kate to the hospital."

Nikolai pulls away. "But I thought—" he stammers. "I thought she was okay," he says to X and then turns back to me. "You cannot leave me again," he says.

I shake my head. "This is all X's doing," I say. "I trust I will be okay soon. But my sister. My grandmother." A tear escapes. "I need to get to them."

In the distance the cellar door grinds open again.

"I will explain everything in the car, Sire," X says, an edge in his voice I do not like. "But we are out of time!"

"I can't walk," I whisper, fear lacing my words. If Adele was happy to find me dead, what will she do if she finds me still alive?

Nikolai stands with me still in his arms, and I wrap mine tight around his neck.

"We cannot exit the cell without being seen," he says.

X raises a brow. "Of course we can, Your Highness. Just not through the door."

CHAPTER EIGHTEEN

Nikolai

X PRESSES A moss-covered stone on the dungeon wall, and it sinks back like a button on a keyboard.

"This palace is full of surprises." He turns with a wink. "Designed that one myself."

Of course I've wondered about X's background story. He is so tight-lipped that it is possible to believe he is anything or anyone. When I came of age he was assigned as my personal bodyguard and soon became my most trusted friend and adviser. I have given him free rein to indulge in any number of curious hobbies from Kenjutsu Japanese swordsmanship to breeding poison dart frogs. But it appears secret passages have also been a keen interest, for I thought I knew them all, and I have just been proved wrong.

"It's a tight squeeze, but it will bring us out at the Gates of Victory," X says.

"And from there we can proceed to the back entrance," I say, unable to believe Kate is still alive in my arms. That this nightmare has turned into a dream.

"The guards in the back keep were sent a flagon of ale from you tonight, as thanks for their service."

"I ordered no such thing," I tell him.

X arches a brow. "I did. And saw it dosed with six seeds of the Evernight Poppy before delivery. The men should be dreaming of busty Edenvale milkmaids this very moment." He glances back at us. "Miss Kate here, however, consumed one entire blossom. She *should* have been out for at least twenty-four hours. I do wonder about that kiss, though…" He trails off.

"What about the kiss?" I ask.

X shakes his head. "Even I don't believe in such tales," he says. "True love's kiss being more powerful than poison? There just is no logical explanation for her early rousing."

I open my mouth to respond, but Kate interrupts me.

"I've never heard of an Evernight Poppy," she murmurs, rubbing my bicep and attempting to shift her body in my arms.

"Of course not," X snaps. "No one outside of a nomadic tribe of Kazakhstani master poison makers knows of the flower's existence." His mouth quirks. "Except me."

Kate attempts to lower herself and take a step but immediately crumples. I sweep her off her feet once more.

"What's happening to me?" Her eyes cloud over with fright. "Why won't my legs work?"

"You were mostly dead. Intermittent paralysis is an unfortunate side effect from the poison."

Kate moans.

"Damn it, X, for how long?" I snarl, hating Kate's fear. She moans again, this time more breathless. "For how fucking long?"

The voices in the corridor grow louder. Whoever is coming for Kate's supposed dead body is almost here.

X beckons me forward and we slip into the secret passage. He pulls a crank and the door slides effortlessly closed. "Not long," he says at last.

"Then why do you look unsettled?" I rumble. The idea of Kate suffering another second more has me in agony.

We wind through the complex twisting labyrinth that X has built through the ancient walls. The corridor is pitch-black except for the powerful flashlight beam that X shines from his wristwatch.

"There is another side effect," he says in a tight voice.

Kate writhes in my arms. "Oh, God," she breathes in a husky whisper unlike any I've ever heard. "Oh, my Jesus God."

I freeze, unwilling to take another step until X fills me in on every last fucking detail.

X sucks in an audible breath. "Unbridled sexual desire is the other effect."

"I need you inside me or I'll die." Kate licks the side of my neck while sliding her hand to cup my bulge. "Feed me that gorgeous royal prick, Your Highness. Inch by majestic inch."

"This side effect, Sire… It won't abate on its own," X says grimly. "It's the poison attacking the part of her brain that controls pleasure."

"I need it so bad," Kate moans. "It hurts. It hurts to want this badly."

My eyes widen. "What do I do?" My cock is granite hard the instant Kate's palm caresses it through my pants. We need to escape, but Kate's sensual moans are making me mad with roaring lust, and soon others will hear her pleas on the other side of the wall.

X turns to regard me in full. His normally inscrutable expression is even harder to read than ever before. "The only cure for this side effect is for someone to bring her to orgasm."

Kate

"X," I growl. "You said I would feel things more keenly in my sleep state." I writhe in Nikolai's arms as we slide through the narrow corridor. "I'm not asleep anymore, and I can't turn it off!" I cry. "The pain is going to kill me!"

I thrash and grind against my prince's hands. "Touch me, Nikolai. God, please, touch me!"

"My apologies, Miss," X says as he leads the way. "The sharp awareness of your senses—of your needs—it is more intense when you wake. And you woke early. You still have much of the drug in your system. Sire, you must pleasure her at once."

"Kate," he says. "I need to know it's not just the drug. I need to be sure that after everything that's happened, you still truly want me like this."

His tortured eyes bore into me, and for one short moment, everything is clear.

"I love you, Nikolai. Of *course* I still want you like this."

"Very well," he says.

My prince repositions me in his arms so that one of his hands is now underneath my dress where I'm wearing nothing at all. A finger grazes my clit and I nearly black out as I scream from the sensation.

"Silence is of the utmost importance," X says, reminding me of our predicament…and that Nikolai and I have an audience.

"Fuck you, X," Nikolai hisses. "You saved her only to torture her?"

We come to a screeching halt, and Nikolai's finger slips inside me. I buck and moan. Nikolai kisses me, no doubt to quiet me, and I'm ravenous for him, teeth gnashing and tongues swirling. I nip at his bottom lip and draw blood, the copper tang filling my taste buds.

A stone door slides open, and we burst into a stairwell and then up and out into the night air.

"Hang in there, Pet. I'm going to take care of you."

But I can't even answer him. I am an animal, biting and scratching in his arms as X flings open the door to the Rolls and Nikolai practically throws me inside. I lie sprawled on my back when he climbs in and kneels beside me. He glances up to the open window where X climbs into the driver's seat.

"Drive!" Nikolai yells, and I feel the car lurch forward.

Tears stream. "Now, Nikolai! Fuck. I need you *now*!"

"As you wish, my lady," he says with a wicked grin.

He shoves my dress up past my hips, spreads my legs wide and plunges two fingers inside me. I cry out in such exquisite agony I think I may burst at the seams. His face disappears between my legs as his tongue assists his fingers, lapping the length of my folds and swirling around my aching clit.

I tear at my hair and writhe along the seat of the Rolls.

"Don't stop! Oh, my God, Nikolai. Don't you fucking stop!" I growl and moan and buck into his face.

And he doesn't stop. He is relentless in his savage

feast—lips, tongue, *teeth* working me to the brink of insanity while his fingers pump inside me.

One of his fingers hits the spot, and his tongue sends me straight over the edge.

I cry out my prince's name as fresh tears stain my cheeks. The relief is overwhelming.

His head collapses between my knees, and for several long moments, no one says a thing.

The car rolls to a stop and X announces our arrival through the still-open divider. "The Royal Hospital of Edenvale," he says. "Shall I give you two a minute?" he asks, not even trying to hide his amusement.

Neither Nikolai nor I say a word. I'm not even sure I've retained the ability to speak.

"And, Miss," X adds. "Congratulations. You're cured."

I wiggle my toes and note that I am no longer paralyzed *or* in sex-starved agony. It would appear that X is correct on all accounts.

"Nikolai?" I say softly when I find my voice again.

He finally lifts his head. His hair is wild and his eyes glazed over.

"Are you truly okay?" he asks.

I push myself to a sitting position and slide my dress back down.

"I'm okay," I assure him. "Thank you."

He runs a hand through his black hair, and I note the weariness in his gray eyes. It finally hits me that I'm not the only one who's endured today.

"I want to make sure *you're* okay," I say. "But—I have to get inside. My sister must be worried sick, and my grandmother…" My voice catches on the word. "She's the reason we needed the money. This was never about deceiving you, Nikolai. Only about saving my family. I should have told you." Tears prick at the backs of my eyes once again.

"Don't worry about me," Nikolai says. "I understand. And I never should have doubted you." His eyes are so tender and full of love. "Whatever you need, Pet. And I'm coming with you."

He reaches for my hand, and I see that the knuckle is split on his own.

"Did you really punch X?" I ask.

His gaze grows dark and all too somber for a moment. "I thought you were dead."

The door opens to my right, and X stands there extending a hand.

"I've a salve for the wound when we get back to the palace, Your Highness." X grins at us, patting his bloodied lip with a silk handkerchief. He closes the door after Nikolai and I exit the vehicle. I marvel at my ability to stand after being paralyzed minutes ago. Then I catch sight of myself in the tinted window of the Rolls and gasp.

Dirt streaks my face, and my hair? I look as if I've been living in the forest like a wild animal.

"You're the most beautiful woman I've ever seen," Nikolai whispers in my ear.

I decide not to chide him for lying because time is everything.

"I have to get in there," I say.

Nikolai laces his fingers through mine. "Let's go."

X leads us inside the main entrance, and it only takes seconds for the gawks and whispers to begin. Before we even make it to the information desk, a camera flashes violently in my face.

"Look!" the paparazzo cries. "It's Prince Nikolai and his latest conquest! How about a quote, Your Highness? Who's the flavor du jour?"

In a flurry of movement, Nikolai has the man by the throat and shoved up against a wall.

"Be careful with your words," he hisses through gritted teeth as the man drops his camera to the floor, his face turning blue.

My eyes widen, and X leans in close, whispering in my ear. "I taught him that."

Before I have time to react, Nikolai lets the man go and is by my side again. In seconds, we've obtained my grandmother's room number. We bypass the elevator and race up the stairs to the fourth floor and stop short just outside her room.

Standing in front of the door are the queen and three guards, Christian and Catriona Wurtzer, and Brother Benedict.

"I almost trusted your little charade," the queen says with a self-satisfied grin. "But imagine my confusion when the prince failed to show up to dinner and I tracked the Rolls to the hospital. Surely X wasn't going to *dispose* of Miss Winter here." She raises a brow. "I suppose I'll have to take care of the disposal myself."

"What the *hell* is this, Adele?" Nikolai growls.

The queen simply nods in our direction. "Arrest them all for treason."

CHAPTER NINETEEN

Nikolai

ONE OF ADELE'S thuggish goons lunges at Kate. But before the oversize gorilla with the neck tattoos can set a single finger on my love's skin, I lay him out with a swift uppercut to the underside of his mean jaw.

"Oof." He hits the floor like a sack of rotten potatoes and doesn't move again.

"That's going to be one hell of a migraine when he comes around," X says with approval, rolling the henchman over with his toe. "Well-played, Sire."

"Who's next?" I roar at the remaining guards. They forget what blood pulses through my veins, that of generations of fierce warriors and plunderers. I am descended from a long and noble line of men and women who got and secured what they wanted by any means necessary. I call on them now to aid me in this hour of dire need. My gut tells me that Nightgardin is using her as their puppet, but I don't have the proof to make an accusation now. Better to wait and watch. For now, the threat is neutralized. She is going down, and Kate will be protected.

Adele snaps her fingers. Sven and Sval, giant twins

who reportedly did time in a Siberian prison as hit men for the Russian mafia, swagger forward, cracking their scarred knuckles.

"Want to tag team, X?" I call out. "A little fun for old times' sake?"

"Only if we challenge ourselves to taking these amateurs in under ten seconds." My bodyguard's wager enrages the twins.

"We *amateurs* eat little worms like you for breakfast." Sven opens his mouth to reveal a row of gold-plated teeth.

"Scared, pretty boy?" Sval jeers.

"I am, actually." I yawn. "Scared that by the time X and I finish with you, there will be nothing left to interrogate."

Sven slowly blinks. "But the queen—"

"Is not heir to the throne." I draw myself to my full height. "And is acting without a signed decree from the royal liege and is therefore in breach of the law. She doesn't have a leg to stand on legally with this attempt at a coup. Treason is being committed here, but it's not by me. With whom do you want to align loyalties, gentlemen?"

"Catriona is not with heir, either!" Christian says, stepping forward, his sister's upper arm in his grasp. "I mean, she's not carrying *your* heir. She made the mistake of confiding her and the queen's little scheme to me. My sister actually thought I'd be party to her own treason to further Rosegate's interests alongside Adele's bigger and more diabolical ambitions. But it's not your child she carries, Nikolai. She has said so herself."

Catriona wrenches from her brother's grasp and

slaps him across the face. "You spoiled everything for me. Everything! The queen will make you pay. *All* of you!"

"I will ruin you," Adele says to my friend, her voice as threatening as the hiss of an adder.

"So be it," Christian says. "But you will *not* ruin the prince." He turns to me. "I'm so sorry, Your Highness. I will never doubt you again." Then he grabs Catriona's arm again and hauls her away.

"Well," I say, eyeing the queen. "That solves the problem of my upcoming nuptials, X. Wouldn't you agree?"

X steps beside me, removing a deadly-looking blade with a jewel-encrusted handle from his black boot. He uses it to casually clean his nails. We are in a hospital, after all, and do wish to remain civil.

"Don't be fools, my good men," I order Adele's remaining brutes. "I am prepared to be reasonable based on the fact you have a combined IQ that is smaller than today's date, but if you come one step closer to Kate, you will be dead." I'll resurrect Edenvale's old beheading customs and do the deed myself.

"Blood doesn't need to be spilled," Benedict breaks in with his deep, commanding voice, as if sensing my murderous urges. A crucifix dangles from his wrist beneath his black clerical habit.

But I am not to be reasoned with. "Anyone here who makes the mistake of touching a single square inch of Kate's body will be chewing on my boot." My voice echoes through the hospital corridor.

The door behind us creaks open.

"Kate?" A fiery-haired woman with creamy skin

and a smattering of freckles peers out. "What's going on? You brought company?"

"Maddie!" Kate sounds on the verge of tears. "Is Gran—?"

"Still touch and go," Maddie says, hugging herself. "She has moments of consciousness, but they are few and far between. Where have you been? You were supposed to relieve me hours ago. I need to step outside for five minutes. Feel fresh air on my face."

"I said arrest them!" the queen shouts to Sven and Sval, but they remain motionless. "Or I shall make sure you are both the first volunteers in my new all-eunuch squadron."

"I must insist that everyone listen to me," Benedict says in a calm voice that silences the chaos. He has always been good at that. "Nikolai has been ordered to marry according to the proclamation, but I have recently learned of the Wagmire Defense."

"The what?" Adele waves her hand. "Never mind— I don't care. Arrest them all."

"If true love can be proven…" Benedict catches and holds my gaze as if the queen hasn't opened her mouth. "Then the marriage may proceed."

Kate gasps behind me.

"Is this true?" I ask, unable to grasp the fact that I might be able to somehow get everything I want.

"I read all eight hundred pages of *The Lesser Known Edenvale Royal Bylaws and Subcommands*." Benedict raises a finger. "There is one catch. To prove true love the couple must swim unassisted across the Bottomless Lake to the Island of Atonement, in accordance with our ancient customs, thereby passing a test of the heart."

I flex my jaw. A mighty challenge awaits us, but I

am determined we shall prove our love's worth. After
so many years in the darkness, I am ready to fight for
this shot at the light.

"Did you just say swim?" Kate asks in a tiny voice
shot through with fear.

An ominous medical device alarm sounds from the
room Maddie has just emerged from. Two nurses run
up the hall. Kate steps forward, the panic on her face
from her fear of water twisting to an expression of
pure anguish.

"Gran, no!"

Kate

The nurses rush past me and nearly knock Maddie out
of the way. The queen and her two guards are forced to
move as well. Nikolai doesn't waste a breath, grabbing
my hand and spiriting me inside the room.

I can't see anything other than the nurses, a flurry of
movement around my grandmother's bed. My breathing hitches as I prepare myself for the worst.

"Sophia," one of them chides, calling Gran by her
first name. "You gave us quite a fright. Next time press
the call button, and we'll be in as soon as you need us."

One of the nurses turns to face my sister and me,
and her eyes widen when she recognizes Nikolai.

"Your—Your Highness. I didn't realize—"

"Ignore me," he commands. "Let the two Miss Win-
ters know what has happened with their grandmother
at once. That should be all that matters here."

Her cheeks redden with embarrassment. "Of course,
Your Highness." She turns to Maddie, the one who's
been here all day. I swallow back the guilt. I should

have come last night when she called. I should have thought about something other than my own fleeting chance at happiness. Then half the ruling body of Edenvale wouldn't be waiting in the hall to take me from my family for good.

"Miss Winter, it seems as if your grandmother is ready to breathe on her own, and she took to telling us by turning off her heart monitor."

Maddie gasps and covers her mouth. I let out a strangled sob.

"She's—she's okay?" I ask, tears of happiness overpowering whatever awaits me when I walk out this door.

The nurse nods, her warm brown eyes immediately setting me at ease. "Please, if you all step out for a few minutes, we can get the doctor in here so we can remove the tube and check her vitals. We'll call you as soon as she's ready."

I nod eagerly, grabbing Maddie's hand. Nikolai holds my other one, and I squeeze them both, two people I love dearly standing beside me.

We step out into the hall, where I find the Royal Police leading away the queen's brutish guards.

"I've spoken with Father," Benedict says to Nikolai. Both men shoot a glance toward Adele, who is also being detained by two officers. "It sounds as if much has gone on tonight that he was unaware of. He'd like to see you for a full statement when you're through here."

Adele growls at us and spits at Nikolai's feet. "You don't deserve happiness," she says. "Not after any chance of it was taken from me because of you and your miserable family. I know people. Powerful people. This is *not* the last you'll hear from me, Prince Nikolai," she vows, her words dripping with both anguish and disdain.

"I'm sure it's not," he says. "But for now I want you out of my sight." He eyes the officers. "Detain her somewhere safe—where she cannot harm others or herself. My father will be in contact with further instructions."

The men nod and take hold of her under the arms, leading her away with heels dragging.

I understand her sadness. I've known great loss, too, as has Nikolai. I'd even shut myself away from the prospect of happiness again after Jean-Luc. For two years I played it safe, afraid to move on. But the queen—she is stuck in a cycle of hate and blame so big that it's blinded her to the world around her.

I shudder.

"No, Pet," I hear Nikolai say. Then my eyes meet his. "I know what you're thinking, and no. I would not have ended up like that."

A tear rolls down my cheek, not only because he's read my thoughts but that he knows what I was thinking about him.

He cups my face in his palms. "It could have been me. I admit that wholly and completely. But it only could have happened had you not walked into my life—or had Adele truly sent you to your death."

He kisses me, his lips fierce and insistent against mine. I can taste the salt of my own tears.

"No," I say. "Your heart may have been dark, but hers is black and cruel. Yours was always salvageable."

"Only by you, Kate."

I smile. "Only by me."

Benedict clears his throat, and I'm reminded that we are not alone.

"The Wagmire Defense," he says.

My grandmother's door opens, and the nurse ushers us in.

"Did someone just say the Wagmire Defense?"

Her voice is like the sweetest music. I keep from throwing myself on her frail body, but I grab Gran's hand and press it to my cheek.

"Yes." I laugh through falling tears. "The Wagmire Defense. Do you—do you know something of it?"

She huffs out a breath as if whatever she's about to say she's told me a million times.

"I knew your mother," she says, and I frown as I realize she's not lucid after all.

"Yes, Grandmother. I know. My mother was your daughter-in-law, remember?"

She waves me off, and the focus of her gaze fixes not on me, not Maddie, but—Nikolai and Benedict.

"I knew *your* mother," she says to the two men. "Knew her when she was a commoner and even after she'd met the terms of the Defense. A great woman, she was—your mother. Pity her history couldn't be shared, sworn to secrecy as we all were."

Nikolai's normally golden skin blanches while Benedict's expression remains impassive.

"She did what she had to do to protect her sons," Gran says, and her gaze returns to me. "And you, my Katie. Love will carry you across the Bottomless Lake. I am sure of it as I'm sure their mother isn't—"

She pauses, and a far-off look takes over her features.

"Nurse," she says, eyeing the woman who's wheeling the ventilator to the other side of the room. The woman turns to face us. "Nurse, would you introduce me to my visitors?"

"We're just volunteers," Maddie says, understanding that Gran's memories have left her. We are once again strangers to her. "Happy to see you're feeling well."

Maddie puts an arm around my shoulders and backs me away from the bed.

"She's gone for now," she whispers. "But it looks like the worst is over."

I nod and swallow back any more tears, for Gran's sake.

"She knew Mother," Benedict says, and I don't miss the hint of bitterness in his voice.

"If your grandmother is telling the truth..." Nikolai starts, but I cut him off.

"She's ill," I tell him. "She could be confusing your mother for someone else."

He shakes his head. "Confusion or not, she knew the Wagmire Defense. Our very own mother found the loophole," Nikolai says softly. "And now Kate—"

I shake my head. "I can't swim," I remind him.

"You can," he says and kisses me. "We can together. And then you'll be my bride."

"I'm terrified," I admit. "And also, that was a terrible proposal. If we survive this Bottomless Lake, I want a real one," I tell him.

He laughs. "And then you'll say yes?"

I shrug but can't fight the giddy smile taking over my face. "I guess we'll see."

He whisks me into the hall, where we hardly have any more privacy, but then, Nikolai loves to put on a show when he has a proper audience. He surprises me, though, with nothing more than a sweet, tender kiss that makes me positively melt.

"I love you," he whispers. "Just so we're clear on that."

I swallow as the words sink in, the words I never thought I'd hear, words he now cannot stop saying. "I love you, too."

"Then that settles it. You *will* be my queen."

I can't help but laugh.

"Still not a proposal," I say.

But yes, I think quietly to myself. *My answer is most certainly yes.*

CHAPTER TWENTY

Nikolai

MY STEPMOTHER IS sent to recuperate on a private thera-
peutic island in the Indian Ocean. Father is still blinded
by his love for her, trusting that her betrayal comes
only from a place of grief. But I know better, as does
X. He promises to continue a private investigation into
Adele's past. Something will turn up.

X briefs me on all the particulars as we race home
at top speed. The Rolls-Royce screeches through the
palace gates. It is time to face Father.

"Pet." I take Kate's hand between mine and kiss each
fingertip. We step out of the car and into the palace's
grand entrance. "X can escort you to my chambers. Ensure you get a proper shower and that the cooks prepare
a batch of fresh scones."

Kate spent some time with her grandmother before
we left the hospital. But now that she is off the ventilator, she and her sister no longer have to remain vigi-
lant at her bedside.

"I don't want to leave you alone to confront your
father," she says, setting her jaw in the stubborn man-
ner that I love.

"I don't need anyone to fight my battles for me," I snap, harder than I intend to.

She is unmoved. "Of course you don't. But you deserve to have the woman who loves you by your side no matter what. In good times and bad."

"My father's temper is worse than mine," I warn.

"I don't scare easily," she says with a small smile. Given that she is still beside me despite everything that has happened, I can only choose to believe her. Love for this amazing woman ignites my veins. She is a spark of everlasting fire. When I am beside her the darkness doesn't stand a chance.

X clicks his heels. "I'll inform air traffic control that we intend to depart for the Bottomless Lake within the hour?"

I nod. "Yes. The sooner the better." I squeeze Kate's hand. "I want you to be mine."

She squeezes back, but then I feel her go rigid.

"Something is wrong," I say.

She worries her bottom lip between her teeth. "Won't it—won't it be dark when we arrive?"

The sun already dips beyond the horizon.

I nod. "Yes. But X will see to it that torches are lit so we can find our way. We can wait until morning, though." I kiss her. "Patience is not one of my finer traits, but I can do it—for you."

She shakes her head. "You're right. The sooner the better. I don't want to chance anything else getting in the way of you being mine, as well." She offers me a nervous smile, and my whole being is set ablaze. What this woman has already risked for me—what she's willing to still chance on my behalf—knocks the air straight out of my lungs. I've never known love like this, and I'm still not sure what I've done to deserve it. She needs to know I'd do the same for her.

I turn her toward me and settle my hands on her shoulders. She seems so delicate. Yet behind that fragility is a strength that threatens to bring me to my knees. "The lake, it is deep beyond measure."

She mashes her lips. "Hence the name."

"I will not force you to swim for me. This kingdom isn't worth making you feel like you're in danger for even a moment."

She swallows. "You'd walk away from all this for me?" Her face is pale even as her blue eyes shine bright.

"Without a second thought," I rumble. "Outside of telling you that I love you, these are the truest words that I have ever spoken."

She dips her head. "You think I'm strong enough for this?"

I tilt her chin up and fix my gaze on her. "I think you are strong enough for *anything*. Never doubt that, Kate. Not for one second, my beautiful, courageous *queen*."

Her eyes glisten, but she holds her head high and smiles. "Then I won't back down. Not an inch. You and I shall rule this kingdom, and I will start demonstrating my future courage as a queen by not letting the Bottomless Lake stand between me and my dreams."

She wraps her arms around my neck and presses her lips to mine. There is the sound of slow clapping.

I glance over, and Father stands in a nearby doorway, studying us with a sardonic expression. "Touching," he says in his deep voice. "The best performance I've seen in years."

Kate

I freeze. Yes, I've spoken to the king before, but it was for business purposes only. His voice hadn't sent ice flowing through my veins then. It does now.

"Don't, Father," Nikolai says, his voice firm, but I'm so attuned to him now that I can hear the strain. The worry.

The prince has his father's eyes, but King Nikolai's irises grow dark as he takes a step toward his son. His salt-and-pepper hair is perfectly in place, his suit tailored to an older yet still ruggedly fit body. If he's any indication of what I have to look forward to as Nikolai ages… I shake my head, banishing the thought. Because other than his distinguished good looks, the king stares at me with utter condescension and disapproval, his own gray eyes mired in distaste.

"How dare you speak to me as such," the man says, standing inches from his son. "How dare you bring your whore into our home when you've broken it beyond repair. The queen is *ruined*, you selfish, ungrateful child."

I gasp. The king opens his mouth to speak again, but Nikolai cuts him off.

"Enough, Father!" he roars, enough so that the man takes a step back. Nikolai's hand still grips mine fiercely, enough so that I feel pain, but I stand my ground along with him. "The true *queen* was my mother. And I know everything. I know about the Bottomless Lake, about the Wagmire Defense, and that my own mother was not of royal blood." He holds up his arm. "Look, Father. Take a good look at where common blood flows through my veins all because you wanted to marry for love. And you dare to deny me the same?"

Nikolai's chest heaves with every breath. All of his words, his passion—it's for *me*.

The king's eyes widen. His skin grows pale, and he stumbles back another step. Yet he says nothing.

"If you ever, *ever* refer to Kate as my whore again, I won't be so kind with you as I was with Adele. She is not fit to be queen, Father. And I think, deep down, you know it. But also know this. If you loved my mother enough to risk the kingdom for her, then you might understand a fraction of what I feel for Kate. We will swim the lake. We will make it to the Island of Atonement. And I will prove that I am worthy of her love."

I take in a sharp breath. "No," I finally interrupt. "Nikolai—I must prove myself to *you*."

He lessens his grip on my hand and brings my palm to his lips, pressing a soft kiss against my skin.

"You never had anything to prove," he said. "You and your sister have given everything of yourselves to take care of the only family you have left. I know this was never about money for you but about unconditional and unwavering love. I've spent too long surrounded by people who are with me for their own gain that I forgot what love was. Perhaps this test of will is meant to prove something to the rest of the royal court, but know that whether we make it to the end of this quest or not, we've already won."

I let out a hiccuping sob, yet my smile is as broad as my love for this amazing man.

I cup his hands in my palms. "We've already won," I echo.

X appears in the doorway behind the king, which is odd considering he should have had to walk past us to arrive there. Then again—as I'm beginning to learn—X is capable of far more than we know.

"Sire. My Lady," he says. "The jet is fueled and ready to go. Are you ready?"

We both nod without hesitation, but the king approaches his son again, this time planting his hands on Nikolai's shoulders. Nikolai stiffens.

"You really love her," he says, and then he begins to laugh. "You *love* her!"

"Father, have you gone mad?"

The king laughs again, his head tilted toward the ceiling. "How," he says, "after all these years, could you expect me to believe your feelings were true? You've never so much as brought a woman to dine with us, yet you are willing to swim the lake for a commoner."

Nikolai's jaw tightens, and his father's laughing ceases.

"Commoner or not, your mother had more royal blood than any queen before her. No one—and I mean *no one*—shall ever be her equal."

Nikolai swallows hard, understanding what I know to be true, as well.

Theirs was a great love—Nikolai's mother and father's. Perhaps that is why someone like Adele was able to manipulate her way to the throne. No one could ever replace the love the king lost, but the kingdom needed a queen. Adele must have been the perfect aristocratic fit—on paper.

But there is so much more to finding the perfect

match, as I've found mine in the most unlikely of places.

"I know the feeling," Nikolai says, the slightest tremor in his otherwise determined voice.

"How did you know?" the king asks, scrubbing a hand across his jaw. "How did you know about your mother?"

I clear my throat. "My grandmother, Your Highness," I say, taking a steady breath. "She's not well, mentally speaking, but she has moments of clarity. I believe she might have known the late queen many years ago."

The king pulls both Nikolai and I into an unexpected embrace, and I respond on instinct, wrapping one arm around each of the men at my sides.

"Go," King Nikolai whispers to us both. "Go prove your love to the rest of the world. You've already proven it to me."

He releases us, and both Nikolai and I bow our heads to our respected ruler.

"Why, though?" Nikolai asks. "Why did you never tell us?"

The king shudders his expression, and I wait for him to repeat what Gran said, something about protecting her sons.

"My father wasn't so understanding," he simply says. "So we were forced to live a lie, to tell all that she came from an ancient royal line only recently uncovered. And because I loved your mother, I didn't fight him on it. She was my queen. That was all that mattered."

It's a nice enough story, but for reasons I cannot explain, I think he's lying. Maybe it's that Nikolai is so much like his father, that being able to read one allows me to read the other.

But Nikolai's beautiful smile is his acceptance, so I let it go. Because Nikolai is my prince. And that's all that matters to me.

"Thank you, My Liege," Nikolai says, and it's in this moment I know he will be the king this country needs...and the man I cannot live without.

As X leads us toward the doors from where we came, Nikolai stops and turns toward his father once more.

"I'd like to move Kate's grandmother—and sister, if she chooses—to the palace after the wedding. Her grandmother will need constant care, so I'll be hiring nursing staff, as well."

His father nods. "Tell me her name, and I'll see to it the preparations are made."

"Sophia Winter," Nikolai says before spinning back toward X so that only I see the look of complete and utter astonishment take over the king's countenance. But it lasts no longer than a second before he is a mask of calm again, so much so that I believe it must have been my imagination playing tricks on me.

"Consider it done," the king says, and before I know it, I'm spirited out the palace gates and to the airfield once again.

"It's time to claim our future," Nikolai says as we stand before the steps leading up to the aircraft.

And then he kisses me until I forget that I almost died tonight, until I forget the king's strange reaction to my grandmother's name, until I forget that I have anything to fear.

I will claim my future, I think, as his tongue sweeps past my lips and I taste victory already.

And then I whisper against him. "My future—is *you*."

CHAPTER TWENTY-ONE

Nikolai

THE BOTTOMLESS LAKE is located in the most remote region on the eastern borders of my kingdom. We fly over fifteen-thousand-foot mountain peaks until we reach a high-altitude meadow with a runway. Long golden grass waves in the wind while white flowers bob as if in greeting. After we disembark the jet, I take Kate's hand in mine, leading the way along the narrow trail. No words pass between us. At least nothing that can be spoken aloud. The trail swings out onto a cliff, and I hear her gasp. Not because of the sheer granite wall and vertigo drop-off. But because of what lies so far down below.

It is the deepest lake in the world. There are rumors of ancient creatures trolling these mysterious waters—sea monsters, mermaids and other such nonsense. But I don't take much stock in the old storytelling.

Still, it's disconcerting to peer into water that blue, visible even in the luminescence of the moon, that pitiless color that seems to attract all available light, to suck it down into its icy heart.

I lace my fingers with Kate's, let our palms slide in

a gentle caress, a delicious promise of later. Heat ignites my veins. Soon, so soon, this beautiful woman will be mine.

X guides us down the stone steps to the lakeshore, and as he sets to work lighting floating torches to blaze our trail, I strip from my clothing in easy, unconcerned movements. As I remove my pants I smile as she stares at my cock.

"See something you like, Pet?" I ask her with a wry smile. I love that my body gives her such wicked, carnal pleasure.

She opens her mouth, and I expect a witty insult. Instead, she sucks in a breath and falls to her knees, bracing her hands on the gravelly beach.

My flirtatious instincts evaporate as I slip into pure protection mode. "What is it?" I drop into a low crouch.

"It's a stupid thing to be this afraid of water, isn't it?" She lifts her gaze, and the pain stamped there almost levels me. "But try rationalizing that with my body."

"Kate, my love, I have told you before, I don't require you to do this. My kingdom pales in comparison to your safety and happiness."

"I want to be brave for you, for me, for us, for love. But it's not the memory of what I've lost at the depths of a river shallower than this. It's what I could lose. I don't just mean us losing our freedom to marry, Nikolai. What if something happened? What if I lost *you*?" Kate shakes her head, and then her jaw takes on that determined set that makes me want her all the more. "Promise me you can do this, and I won't let fear win." She removes her dress and is bare before me, all creamy skin and soft angles. Her perfect breasts make my mouth water.

I step forward. "I can do this, Kate. *We* can do this. Though I can't help feeling that I don't deserve you."

She presses a cool hand to the side of my cheek, skimming my stubble. "We could stand here debating that claim, or we could swim to the Island of Atonement and get on with the rest of our lives."

We stare out to the middle of the lake, now dotted with small licks of flame, to where a modest, heart-shaped island is covered by a thick blanket of trees. In the middle is a tall stone tower, glittering in the brilliant moonlight, that looks as ancient as the mountains.

"What is waiting for us out there?" she whispers.

"I can't say for certain." I cover her hand with mine. "But whatever dangers or mysteries we are about to face, we'll face them together."

"Just as we will anything else in life."

She nods and wades into the water, and I've never seen anything more stunning. This woman is willing to sacrifice anything for me, for us.

I feel the same way.

And so I follow after.

Kate

The water is surprisingly warm, yet I inhale a shuddering breath. Nikolai's hand is still in mine as we wade deeper, following the line of X's torchlights, though X himself is nowhere to be seen.

Because we must do this alone.

Nikolai suddenly halts.

"What is it?" I ask.

He squeezes my hand. "The bottom will drop out soon," he warns, and I can tell he fights to keep his voice even. "You said once that your sister said you could swim, that you'd just blocked it out. I can't let you go any farther, Kate. Not if you are putting your life at risk."

I nod, knowing what he is asking of me—what I am asking of him. The water is halfway up my torso, my breasts nearly covered, and despite the balmy air, I tremble. Then I squeeze my eyes shut and drop beneath the surface, letting go of Nikolai's hand. The last thing I hear is him frantically calling my name.

I force my eyes open. The water is clear but dark, and in the places below a floating torch, I catch the movement of a fish or whatever else dwells beneath the surface. My heart races as panic threatens to take hold of my senses, but I remind myself that there is clean air above me, that I am not alone, and that I am not trapped as my parents were.

I am not trapped. But Nikolai is. And he is depending on me to set him free.

I kick my legs out behind me and push my palms and my outstretched arms through the water. And then I burst through the surface. My feet no longer reach the ground, yet I am still here. I am in control.

I am triumphant.

"Kate!" Nikolai cries, his voice hoarse as he swims out to meet me. "Fucking hell, Kate. What are you doing?"

I grin as my arms and legs make circles through the inky blue. "I'm pretty sure I'm swimming," I say, and my heart thunders in my chest. "Oh, my God, Nikolai. I'm swimming!"

His eyes gleam silver in the moonlight, and the terror I know I caused washes from his face.

"You did it," he says. "Jesus, fuck, you did it!"

I narrow my eyes. "Don't let Benedict hear you speaking like that."

He lets out a broad, bellowing laugh and kisses me as he keeps himself afloat.

"Let's go get our future," I say. He nods, and we set out for the island.

We swim from torch to torch, each one a beacon. As my adrenaline wanes and the long minutes set in, my limbs grow weary.

"Just make it to the next torch," Nikolai says, when he senses my exhaustion.

And so I vow to make it to the next torch. And then the next one. And the one after that until I stumble as my toes unexpectedly dig into sand.

I straighten and stand as tears spring from my eyes. Nikolai doesn't waste a second as he scoops me into his arms and kisses me hard, unrelenting, and I realize my only fear now is that I will never be able to get enough of this man.

He doesn't let go, doesn't release me from the kiss as he strides onto shore, his strong arms holding me close. It is a mirror image of the day we met, when he carried me to safety in the maze. Then I was determined to marry him off to another. But today I risk everything to make him mine.

I cling to his solid, naked form as he marches straight for the stone monument, and he only releases me when we stand before a carved-out doorway that beckons us to enter.

We do.

I gasp as Nikolai whispers, *"Look."* His head tilts toward the ceiling—or at least where there should be one. But instead the stone opens to the star-speckled sky, to the full moon in all her brilliance, lighting us from above. I spin, my eyes taking in the walls that surround us, and see that they are covered with rich, painted murals, all different versions of two lovers discovering this land.

"Oh, Nikolai." Those are my only words, though. I am not sure I have breath to give life to what I wish to say.

"I know," he says, relieving me from the burden as we simply marvel and stare.

I run my hands along the painted stone walls until I come to a spot of empty canvas, a section of a wall waiting for the next painting. It's then that my fingers nick a loose stone, sending it crashing to the floor.

I gasp. "I'm sorry! Oh, my God. I broke the monument. I survived that swim to come here and ruin this sacred place, and I—" But I gasp again as Nikolai, without hesitation, reaches his arm inside the shadowy opening. This is the thing horror stories are made of, and I brace myself for him to cry out as some deadly creature takes his hand, but instead he pulls out a blue wooden box no bigger than a schoolchild's pencil case. A piece of parchment is wrapped around it, fastened with a waxen seal.

Now it is Nikolai who gasps.

"What is it?" I ask, and he stares up at me, his gray eyes glistening.

He smiles as a tear escapes down his beautiful, chiseled cheek.

"This is the royal seal," he says. "I think—I think this is from my parents."

I step into his grasp, wrapping my arms around his torso. Then he breaks open the seal and unfolds the parchment, holding it up for both of us to see.

"Read it to me," he says. "I'm too fucking nervous."

I swallow and do as he asks, reading the letter aloud as my own eyes well with tears again.

To Our Dearest Nikolai,

Generations have gone before us, those that have abided by the ancient decree. And should you go that route as well, we pray that you are happy. That if and when it is necessary, this finds your heir; that generations do not pass before Edenvale is rewarded once again with a king and queen who are pure of heart. For we have found the way to true happiness.

Our only hope is that you are able to do the same. Should you find the one who fills your heart, then she shall also be the one to fill your soul. There is no room for blackness, for hate, for anything to cloud the mind of a king who shall rule with a just hand if he has true love in his heart. If you've found this gift, do not take such treasure for granted. Populate the palace with heirs, with products of a love immeasurable, and the kingdom will prosper as does your devotion.

To love and be loved in return—there is no greater reward we can bestow upon you. But take what is in this box and use it as a token of that love. Then, when the time is right, come back to this place and paint your story upon these walls. Leave a token for those who come after you.

With all the love in our hearts, King Nikolai and Queen Cordelia

I wipe away tears as I finish, my arms still around my prince. He says nothing as he opens the box and removes a glorious sapphire-and-diamond ring—a ring fit only for a queen.

He pulls away and stares down at me with shining eyes, his beautiful naked body bathed in radiant moonlight. He lets the box and parchment clatter to the stone floor as he drops to his knee.

"You said you wanted a real proposal," he says, no hint of the rogue I met barely a month ago in his gaze or in his tone.

I cover my mouth and nod, unable to speak without the possibility of sobbing.

"Then here it is, Kate. There is nothing more real than my love for you. Words cannot capture it. The entire kingdom cannot contain it. It is as deep as a lake with no bottom and as vast as the infinite universe. I would have given up my birthright for you, but instead you gave up your fear for me. I can think of no greater act of love than the one you have performed. I beg you to give me a lifetime to repay you. Be my life. Be my love. Be my queen."

I sink to my knees in front of him, pressing my lips together to keep from falling apart. Then I stand and take his face in my hands.

"Yes," I whisper, and I kiss him again and again and again. "Yes, Nikolai." He kisses me back, pulling my

left hand free so he can slide the ring onto my finger.
It is a perfect fit. "Infinite times—*yes*. But wait. First
we have to take care of one pesky detail."

His face blanches. "What. What more do you need?
Kate, I'll do anything to win your hand."

I take a step toward him, splaying my palms against
his chest. "We had a wager."

And there it is, that feline grin of his that tells me
he wants to devour me whole. I might let him.

"Why, yes, my love. We did have a wager. And I do
believe you won. Didn't you?"

I nod. "Do you remember the terms?"

His brows furrow, and he scrubs a hand across his
beautifully stubbled jaw. "I owe you nothing more than
a favor. Would you like me to make payment? What
is your price?"

I nod again then stand on my toes and whisper in
his ear. Nikolai's eyes widen, and he lets out a guttural sound.

"As you wish, Beloved," he says.

My skin is pebbles of gooseflesh. I'm wearing nothing but the glittering jewels on my finger. I marvel at
his stiff length, ready for me as the heat coils in my
belly, so very ready for him. I let him guide me back
into the water. He speaks no words at all as he pulls
me over his beautiful body.

The lake water is cool against my skin, but his tip
is warm and wet at my opening where he nudges until
slick heat envelops his perfect, thick erection. I sink
over it, burying him to the hilt.

He bites my shoulder and growls.

I slide up slowly and let him swirl around my swollen center before plummeting over him again.

He cradles my face in his hands and stares intently into my eyes—eyes I know are reddened from tears of disbelief, of love, of complete and utter joy.

"We may rule this kingdom for a lifetime, but you—my future wife and my future queen—shall rule my heart for eternity. Just as those paintings on the island's tower wall, my love for you lives beyond this life and beyond this world."

"Nikolai," I gasp as he moves inside me. "I love you, too."

"But," he says, flicking his tongue against my lips, the devil in his stare, "just because you rule me doesn't mean you'll ever tame me."

He pinches my pebbled nipple, and I shriek at the exquisite pleasure and pain.

"After all—I'm still one royal prick."

And he is my royal temptation. I will never, ever get enough.

EPILOGUE

X

I WIPE REMNANTS of drywall from my shoulder as the sound of drilling whines through the ceiling.

"You're getting sloppy, X," she scolds from the shadows. "You've been followed."

I step to the left and watch the drywall dust on the carpet to my right.

I raise my brows, knowing that she can see me even though I cannot see her.

"Really?" I ask. "Because if that were true, why are they a floor above?" I nod toward the flashing blue light on the desk in front of her. "Perhaps they have no idea *I'm* here. Perhaps they weren't even looking until a server signal popped up on their screen." I imagine her dark eyes boring holes through me.

She lets out a sigh. "You are still as arrogant as ever."

I grin and take a step forward. She doesn't stop me because she knows I'm still not close enough to see.

"And you're still as easy to ruffle as ever. And, my Lady, I do enjoy ruffling you."

There is a long silence but for the drilling overhead.

They will break through soon. We're on borrowed time, but then again, we always are.

"Tell me," she says, her voice firm, though I detect the slightest tremor. Our parrying is over. "Is he safe?"

I open my mouth to say her name—or maybe her call sign, *D*. But I stop myself as I always do. If I don't speak it aloud, no one else can hear. If I don't see her in the flesh, they cannot torture her existence from me.

I bite back a self-satisfied grin. I've survived the worst any captor has had to offer—whips, brands, knives sharp enough to draw blood yet small enough that bleeding out would be a long, slow death.

Much to the disappointment of all who've tried, I'm not dead. Unfortunately for them—they are.

"X," she pleads, as if I'd ever falter on a mission.

"He is safe," I say. "He and the princess are enjoying an extended honeymoon on a private island off the coast. They will return soon, but plans for the celebration have been postponed until the king decides what to do with the traitorous queen. The prince, though, will rule at his father's side, and the princess will serve as ambassador to our neighbors."

"And Rosegate?" she asks.

A chunk of ceiling falls to the floor.

"We don't have much time," I say. "They *will* break through. And Rosegate is secure for the time being, but we're still trying to figure out if the queen's motive was merely to take the throne or to aid Nightgardin in Edenvale's fall."

She pulls the thumb drive, the source of the flashing light, from the laptop's USB port.

"We won't be here when they break through," she says, and I hold up my palm, my hand curling into a fist to catch the small projectile. "I want the oldest prince to remain under surveillance, but you are relieved of immediate duty when it comes to him."

I nod. More drywall falls. I clip the carabiners to the belt loops on my trousers and wonder for the first time if the material will hold. I guess we're about to find out.

"What is the next mission?" I ask, knowing there is one.

I hear the wheels of her chair roll and can tell from the cadence of her breathing that she's now standing.

"It's all on the drive," she says.

I look down at the blue light in my palm. "The heir spare," I say, knowing without a computer monitor in front of me to corroborate. This is exactly what Nikolai wanted anyway. He will be none the wiser when my attentions shift.

"He is lost," she says, "the second son." Her voice grows distant as she does what she does best and disappears into a world that used to recognize her in seconds— one that now knows nothing of her existence.

Lost, I think. *What if he doesn't want to be found?*

The ceiling caves in, and because being found is not on *my* agenda for the day, I unhook one of the carabiners and leap from the fifteenth-floor window.

I throw the bungee cable over the line and let gravity and the southerly wind do their job.

I skim over taxis, buses, locals and tourists, none of them aware of my existence overhead.

When I land on the hotel balcony, I make a mental note to thank the tailor of this suit. The strength of the belt loops is exquisite.

I brush away any further signs of ceiling dust and pick up my tumbler from the balcony ledge, draining the rest of my scotch. Then I thrust open the balcony doors to find a delicious brunette naked on the bed, a blindfold over her eyes and her wrists still bound to the bedpost. She purses her luscious, red-painted lips into a pout.

"You said you were running out to grab your drink. You've been gone for at least five minutes, X."

I check my watch. "Seven, darling."

She writhes against the satin sheet and bites her lip. "Well, I'm counting the minutes until you fuck me."

I tap my breast pocket and make sure the flash drive is stored securely. Then I tear off the jacket.

"Spread your legs and count down from three," I command, and she writhes again.

I unbutton my shirt.

"Three," she moans.

I lose the pants.

"Two."

I press my knees into the edge of the bed and run a hand up her thigh, my thumb teasing her folds where I left her drenched with anticipation.

"One," she whimpers.

Time's up.

* * * * *

Keep reading for a sneak peek at
Benedict's story
MY ROYAL SIN
Coming soon!

Ruby

You have one month to break him, to make sure he does not take his vows still a virgin.

The door from the stairwell starts to slide open, and because I have no choice, I sneak past the pews and into a confessional. I'm still trying to calm my breathing when the shadow of a man appears on the other side of the lattice.

"Have you come to make confession?" a deep, gravelly voice asks.

I stopped believing in any higher power long ago. But I know why I'm here and what part I need to play. "Forgive me, Father. For I have sinned."

I open the screen on my phone that has my script for the evening and hope on my brother's innocence that giving up my own will set him free. If I can earn the money Madam promised, then I can buy the best legal representation in the kingdom and set my brother free.

"You may proceed, child," he says. "The Lord is ready to forgive your sins."

I stroke a finger along the lattice grate and remind myself to play the part for which I'm being paid.

"What if I want to keep sinning?" My voice is breathy and soft as I infuse it with the need a client would ache to hear. I glance at the screen in my palm.

"What if all I want is to relieve you of that desire pulsing between your legs?"

He hisses in a breath. "Who sent you?" I can tell he speaks between gritted teeth.

"Let me taste your thick, aching cock, Father," I say, my voice sweet as an angel as I try not to sound like I'm reading. "Let me take you so deep. I want to feel you throbbing, salty sweet against my tongue—"

"Who. Sent. You?" he interrupts, but I will not be deterred, not when my only choice is to succeed.

I scroll through the preplanned dialogue on the screen. "Think of all those times you've come alone," I tell him. "Every fantasy you've ever had, every sinful act you've dared let yourself imagine—I can be that for you."

His breaths are ragged, but he does not speak.

I let go of the lattice and slip my free hand under my skirt.

"Sire." I moan, as I slip a finger beneath my thong, working myself until I'm wet. "Do you hear that?" I ask, plunging two fingers into my now-slick heat. "That's my pussy, so ready for you. Don't you want a taste, Sire? Just a little lick?"

You need the money.

This silent reminder plays in my head as I try to lose myself in pleasure.

This is for your family.

I swirl a slippery finger around my clit and gasp, the phone clattering to the floor. "Don't. You want. To make. Me. Come?" I ask between gasps, the words all me now. I am lost in the moment. "Is your hand on that cock, Sire? Is it daring you to bury yourself inside me? Because all you have to do is step outside that booth and sheathe yourself to the hilt."

I try to bring myself to climax, but even I can't forget entirely where I am or why I ended up here. So I embellish, crying out in feigned ecstasy.

"Oh... Your Highness. Oh God! Your Highness, I can't—" I add a few more gasps before yelling, "Benedict!"

"Enough!" he growls, and I collapse back onto my knees with a satisfied grin.

Yes. That was quite enough.

He waited until he thought I was done, which means he didn't want me to stop. If that's all that comes of tonight, I have succeeded in the first step.

Because this is not just any client on the other side of the wall. He is a prince, second in line for the throne and brother of our future king. I startle to see him standing in the opening of my booth.

"Forgive me, Father," I say, straightening the skirt that barely covers what lies beneath. The air smells of sex, and the man looming before me stares with beautiful green eyes. "Did I make you sin?"

LET'S TALK
Romance

For exclusive extracts, competitions
and special offers, find us online:

f facebook.com/millsandboon

◎ @millsandboonuk

𝕏 @millsandboon

Or get in touch on 0844 844 1351*

For all the latest titles coming soon, visit
millsandboon.co.uk/nextmonth

Want even more
ROMANCE?

Join our bookclub today!

'Mills & Boon books, the perfect way to escape for an hour or so.'

Miss W. Dyer

'Excellent service, promptly delivered and very good subscription choices.'

Miss A. Pearson

'You get fantastic special offers and the chance to get books before they hit the shops'

Mrs V. Hall

Visit millsandbook.co.uk/Bookclub
and save on brand new books.

MILLS & BOON